The Three Presidents

An Adam Galloway Adventure

Timothy D. Holder

Cover art by Jill Holder

ISBN 979-8-9866410-4-1

Chapter One

I knew that, ultimately, I was the only one responsible for my attitude. I knew that my mood did not have to be dictated by my circumstances; it was my choice and my responsibility to decide how I would process my experiences. And that all sounded good, but in the moment, I was having a hard time not giving in to a surly disposition. As far as I was concerned, this day was going terribly.

I had no idea how dramatically worse it was about to get.

My current bad attitude was the result of having to walk a half mile in the rain from my house to that of my father-in-law. Not only was I getting drenched, but my vision problems were extremely frustrating. I had been through a lot in eighteen years of active service in the Navy, but at least I had never had eye problems. Ironically, I had recently ended up in the wrong place at the wrong time on a Navy Reserve weekend and been victimized by a couple of careless idiots with a flashbang grenade and a box of fireworks.

I had thanked God more than once that my vision was not permanently impaired, but my eye doctor insisted that I wear ridiculously oversized and extra dark sunglasses for a few more weeks. I wasn't convinced the eye doctor knew what he was talking about, but I figured it was better to be safe than sorry.

The problem was that the clouds, rain, and fancy sunglasses made it difficult to see where I was going. Thus, in addition to getting waterlogged, I was convinced that I was going to trip at any moment and end up rolling down the hill my daughter and I were walking across.

But that was not really the worst of it. No, the worst part of the day was that I was going to my father-in-law's house to accept the man's job offer.

It would have been nice to know what the job was, but Fred Perkins hadn't bothered to explain himself, and I was too proud to demand information. I had wanted to just say no. The best I could do was wait a couple of days to respond, but I couldn't put it off any longer. I was desperate—I needed an income, and Fred was successful enough as a toy inventor that he could pay.

But for what exactly?

I'd spent the best years of my life serving my country. I had faced long stretches away from the family I loved. I'd survived deprivation and literal torture.

Fred invented toys for a living. Who does that? Kris Kringle?

My daughter Liz noticed my loud, long exhale of frustration. She side-eyed me and said, "I told ya you should've brought an umbrella."

"Thanks for the reminder."

"Yep, I sure am dry under my umbrella," she said in a singsong voice. "Nothing like an umbrella to keep you dry on a rainy day."

"Stop. Saying. 'Umbrella.'" I growled.

"Sorry, Daddy!" she said in a totally insincere voice. She laughed and added, "Last one to Grandpa's is a 'Nolan Galloway.'" She took off running.

Years ago, Liz had started substituting her brother's name for "rotten egg." She was a funny kid.

She was sixteen, but sometimes when I looked at her, it was hard not to see the three-year-old she used to be. There were other times when a conversation with her was like talking to another adult. But maybe not so much when she was giving me a hard time while I was getting soaked in the rain.

I jogged after her, even though I had read somewhere that a person gets wetter from running in the rain than walking. It seemed counterintuitive, but I had always believed it. I jogged through the downpour anyway so I could keep up with Liz. It increased the likelihood that I might trip and fall, but I figured I would risk it. I would rather look clumsy than timid in front of my daughter.

The main problem was not getting wetter or tripping, it was that jogging would get me to Fred's house quicker than walking would. And that house was the one place I did not want to be.

Fred Perkins might be a genius inventor and doting grandfather to the rest of my family, but to me, Fred was an arrogant and impossible to please father-in-law. I did not want to work for him, because he'd expressed nothing but disappointment with me and my career choices so far. I was loathe to go to the man with hat in hand, but my last two career moves had been disasters. The fact that Fred had been proven correct about my choices drove me even further up the wall. Fred was not a gracious winner.

But now it was time to swallow my pride and be a provider for my family. I was not happy with the idea of Elaine having to carry the financial burden alone.

Liz and I approached Fred's yard from the rear and jogged around his obnoxiously high fence. When we came to the front, Liz punched in the security code on the gate, and we entered Fred's yard. We jogged the length of the driveway and up the steps to Fred's lavish, three-story house, then Liz knocked on the front door.

Suddenly, my military-honed situational awareness began to kick in. The door opened, but I hadn't heard anyone walking up to it on the other side. Fred's wood floors produced a lot of noise, but there was no sound. It was as if someone was standing there waiting for us. Fred knew we were coming over, but he would've already opened the door if he was standing right inside. It was as if someone was just waiting for us to knock, but why do that?

The door opened, and the man inside was instantly recognizable, yet I couldn't place where I knew him from. The stranger was not one of Fred's employees. Fred had an assistant named Templeton and a husband-and-wife team that cleaned, cooked, and ran errands, but even with my flawed vision, I knew this man was not one of them. There were no cars in the driveway—not even the employees' cars, which was strange. The man at the door seemed to be in his late fifties, and he had his slightly receding hair combed back. He wore a dark, conservative suit.

The stranger did a doubletake when he saw me. "You're soaked," the man said. "You should have brought an umbrella."

"Good idea," I said flatly.

Liz chuckled as she set her own umbrella out of the way.

I wiped water off myself as best I could, standing at the top of the steps and flicking my hands out into the yard so I wouldn't drench Fred's fancy entranceway.

"What's with your eyes?" the stranger asked. "Are you blind or something."

I was taken aback at the man's brusque, insensitive question and its matching tone. I knew my oversized dark sunglasses tended to attract notice, and sometimes people stared, but it was usually just young children who asked questions so bluntly.

"Navy Reserve training," I answered, because why not? Just because the stranger was rude, it didn't mean that I had to be. "I got my vision messed up. It's temporary."

The man responded with a single nod of his head and an inarticulate noise. He seemed devoid of sympathy or even common courtesy. But I surmised that the man was not so much mean as he was socially inept.

"Who are you?" asked Liz. Her question was a little blunt, but she was clearly as surprised as I was by the man's presence at the door. And if he was comfortable dishing out direct questions, then he couldn't really complain about receiving them.

Nevertheless, the man seemed to be caught off guard and even irritated by the question. "Who am I? I'm the president," he grumbled.

"Of what?" I asked.

"Of the United States, Genius."

"I'm...not convinced you really think I'm a genius." I was not above fighting sarcasm with sarcasm. "And you don't look anything like the President of the United States."

The man looked at me as if I was an idiot. "I'm Richard Nixon."

My eyes widened. That's why he looked so familiar. The man was a dead ringer for Nixon, but that would be crazy. Nixon had died many years earlier, and this guy resembled Nixon during his presidential years, which was more than a half-century ago.

Of the multiple questions that suddenly leapt to mind, the most pressing one was, *What have you gotten into, Fred?*

Chapter Two

"If you're really Richard Nixon," I said, "shouldn't you be more, um, dead?"

Nixon shook his head and waved his hands. "I'm sure you have a lot of questions, but I don't care because there's information we need, and it might not be safe out here in the open."

Liz looked as confused as I felt.

Nixon peered over and around me and Liz. She and I looked at each other, then began imitating the stranger, turning this way and that, looking for we knew not what.

Despite my efforts to look around, I never took my eyes off Nixon for more than one second at a time. This situation was weird, and I did not like weird situations.

"You should come inside," Nixon said.

"Where's my Grandpa?" Liz asked. "He texted me to come see him, and Dad had to talk to him too, so we came over together."

"Yeah, I'm the one who texted you. I used his phone"

"Wait…what?" I said.

"Look," replied Nixon, "it's not safe to do this out here. They might come back."

"Who might come back?" Liz asked. "Where's Grandpa? I want to see him right now."

Liz was clearly getting frustrated, and I was getting impatient too. "Okay, Mr., um, Nixon, I think you'd better step out here on the porch and start explaining things. Who are you, and where is Fred?"

My impulse was to grab the guy by the collar and drag him out into the front yard, but I was afraid I might break his neck. I had done so much training over the years that the greatest challenge was not in winning a fight; it was in figuring out how to not hurt someone too badly. This Nixon guy had no way of knowing it, but not only had I received combat training in the Navy, I was also a serious student of the martial arts. I earned a junior black belt in Tae Kwon Do in high school, and I got another black belt in Wing Chun when I was in college.

"So you're the dad. Yeah, I figured that when I saw you. Those weird glasses just distracted me."

"Congratulations. Now step out here and answer my question."

"I've got a better idea," Nixon said.

He lunged forward and grabbed Liz by both her arms. He hauled her into the house and kicked the door shut behind himself.

My jaw dropped at the horror of it. I took a half second and consciously set aside my concern for Nixon's safety. After leaving the Service, I assumed I would never be in a situation where I would have to seriously hurt someone. But this Richard Nixon doppelganger had changed that. He had just taken Liz.

I was ready to kill.

I took a step towards the front door. I pivoted halfway around, bent my knee, and drew my leg up. I lashed out and slammed my foot into the front door next to the knob. It almost broke.

Not the door, but my foot. I almost broke my foot trying to kick open the door.

Leave it to Fred Perkins to have his front entryway super reinforced.

I yelled in pain, but more so in frustration. I grabbed the doorknob with both hands and twisted as hard as I could. I almost lost my grip because I was trying to turn the knob with much more force than was necessary.

The door was unlocked.

I had almost broken my foot on an unlocked door.

"You have got to be kidding me," I muttered under my breath, as I pushed open the door and limped inside.

I was ready to attack Nixon, but Liz beat me to it. Nixon had let go of her and stepped back, but she moved forward and smacked the presidential wannabe on the arm.

"Ow!" he yelled and moved away even further to escape her wrath.

"You really had that coming, Richard. And you probably deserved worse for manhandling that poor girl."

I turned to the voice, and out of the corner of my eye, I saw Liz do the same. I heard a gasp, and I honestly was not sure if it was Liz who made the noise or if it had escaped from my own mouth.

There was a man standing on the staircase, five steps from the bottom with a hand on the rail. He was tall and thin and wore an old-fashioned suit. Really, the plain-looking, bearded man was unremarkable in every way except one.

He was a dead ringer for Abraham Lincoln.

Chapter Three

I took a breath to collect myself. Then I took another.

"Liz? Honey? Are we standing in Fred's living room with Richard Nixon and Abraham Lincoln."

"Um…y-yes, sir."

"Good. At least I'm not hallucinating. Let's call that a win."

"Miss Liz, it is a privilege to meet you," said the man who looked like Lincoln. "I don't suppose I need an introduction." He smiled at her, but his benevolent look morphed into confusion as he turned his attention to me.

"And who might you be, good sir?"

"I'm Adam Galloway, and I'm looking for my father-in-law."

"If you will pardon me for saying so, I'm not sure how you can look for anyone."

"He's not blind, he just has bad eyes…and weird glasses," said Nixon.

I sighed.

Using my foot to shut the door allowed me to keep Liz and the men in my field of vision. I stepped further into the room, which brought me closer to both presidents.

"I came here looking for Fred Perkins, and all I've found are a couple of freaks playing dress up. Now either you tell me where Fred is, or I start knocking a couple of presidential heads together."

Lincoln stuck his hands in front of himself, palms facing out—the universal gesture for "take it easy." He said, "Please stop acting so agitated, sir. You're about to give me a case of the hypo."

"Fred?" I yelled. I waited a beat, then called out his name a second time. No response.

Lincoln spoke again, "Miss Liz, the answers you and your father seek are upstairs. At least, that's where you will get the answers such as we have them."

He turned to ascend the stairs to the second floor, and Nixon headed in the same direction.

Lincoln peered back down at us. "You might want to help your father navigate these steps, my dear. We don't want him to fall."

Liz awkwardly looked back and forth—from the presidents to me—then we headed after the two strange men. When Liz and I were side by side, I whispered, "I'll show him someone falling down the steps. I'll bounce that hairy baboon down here headfirst if we don't find out what's going on."

I wasn't worried about Liz's safety. I didn't imagine these presidential impersonators were better martial artists than I was, and I was carrying a gun.

"We need to find Grandpa. I don't care why those guys look the way they do. I just want Grandpa."

"Um…yeah…sure." My eyeroll was hidden by my dark glasses, but Liz wasn't looking at me anyway. Not knowing what was going on made me irritated, but as far as I was concerned, Fred had gotten himself messed up in something, and now we were getting dragged into it.

We made our way up the stairs and came to the hallway that bisected the rooms on the second floor. Pictures of Grandpa with the kids, Grandpa with Elaine, Grandpa with his late wife, and Grandpa with various friends, customers, and even a few dignitaries all lined the two walls. Really, there were pictures of everyone that one might imagine would be hanging there with good ol' Grandpa. Everyone, that is, except for me.

What Liz didn't realize was that the customers and dignitaries only had their pictures taken with Fred because he made a few popular toys, and he had money. To everyone but Elaine and the kids, Fred was a jerk.

Lincoln and Nixon led us to the third door on the right, opened it, and went inside.

Liz and I shared a frown. That room had always been locked for the entire twenty years I'd known Fred. The old toy inventor always dismissed it as a closet for the storage of half-done inventions and proprietary secrets.

I had just assumed that the man was hiding his failures there.

Clearly, I was wrong. But just as clearly, Fred had been lying.

Liz and I stopped in our tracks once we reached the room.

"Dad," Liz stage whispered. "It's Teddy Roosevelt."

Sure enough, there he was, sitting at a computer desk awkwardly located in the middle of the room.

"Of course, it is. Why wouldn't we walk into a room with Teddy Roosevelt typing on a computer?"

Lincoln and Nixon flanked the newest president who slowly rose to his feet.

"Excellent! We have the girl here now," said Roosevelt. "Good work, Richard. Bully!"

Chapter Four

"I have no idea what's going on here, but the one thing I know for sure is that you most definitely do not have the girl."

"You must be the father," said the Roosevelt lookalike. "Let me assure you, as one father to another, we mean your daughter no harm. In fact, our primary concern is to keep her safe."

I stalked into the room, clenching and unclenching my fists. I scanned my environment, cataloging potential threats. There were no other doors through which bad guys might enter. There were two windows, but we were on the second floor, so they didn't seem to be anything to worry about. There were several cabinets lining the walls that were big enough to hide a grown man, but that was just weird thinking on my part. Probably.

The room seemed safe to me, except, maybe, for the three guys who looked like presidents.

Admittedly, I was a little distracted by also wondering why Fred had misled us. There were no half-finished, failed inventions in here unless they were hidden away in the cabinets. Why had Fred locked off the area and lied about it for so long?

I pushed these thoughts out of my mind.

"Liz, we're so glad you are here," a huge grin spread across Roosevelt's face.

I ignored the man's rudeness—I was standing right next to Liz, but they weren't glad to see me? Instead, I focused on my more immediate concern.

"Okay," I said, "Three middle-aged men should never be this happy to see my sixteen-year-old daughter. Stop talking about her and tell me where Fred Perkins is, or I'm going to lose my sunny disposition."

It was not an idle threat, which made it all the more surprising that Roosevelt ignored me.

The Bull Moose President looked at Liz, "We're— how shall I explain this? I suppose I will just be succinct since we have such a situation as we do. Your grandfather is more of an amazing inventor than he let on, young lady. He...created us." He paused for just a moment, presumably so Liz could process that revelation.

I couldn't quite wrap my head around the words. "So...like...Fred's a makeup artist in his spare time? He grew you three in a test tube? What do you mean?"

The three presidents glanced back and forth awkwardly. "You might refer to us as artificial," said Roosevelt.

"You're telling me you're robots?" I was stupefied.

"We're androids." Nixon answered without looking at me. He only had eyes for Liz, but not in a weird way, which was lucky for him.

"Our personalities come from computer programs based on the historical records of the things we wrote, our speeches, and what our contemporaries wrote about us. Our speech patterns and vocabulary have been modernized a little to make us more easily understood," said Roosevelt

"Unfortunately," Lincoln interjected, "we have a problem. In fairness, we have two problems."

"We shouldn't work," mumbled Nixon with his eyes downcast.

"Wait a minute," Liz said, "This is blowing my mind. I mean, it really is, but where's Grandpa? He should be here. Do you know where he is?"

"Don't get upset," Lincoln said, "but he's been taken."

"And we shouldn't work," Nixon repeated, shaking his head.

"No," Liz said. "You have to work. You can't just sit around. Grandpa needs you! You have to tell us where he is."

Roosevelt smiled kindly. "That's not what he meant, dear girl. Our technology does not work properly. We should not be functioning. I read it all on the computer screen."

"Maybe Fred's just..." My voice trailed off. I could not bring myself to argue that Fred was a bigger genius than they realized.

If Fred had been here, he would have made that argument himself.

Roosevelt shook his head. "What I was reading was his journal. He wrote that he had two big problems he could not get around. He said that our movements were too jerky and robotic. Also, our computer programs could not interact with incoming stimuli fast enough. In response to comments he had or movements he made in his interactions with us, it took our programs too long to determine a reasonable response for us to make. And he recorded his entry yesterday, so he hardly had time to address both issues. We should not be working—walking and talking like normal people—but we are. There's only one explanation for this." Roosevelt paused.

Liz and I looked at each other again. Nobody said anything. First, we find out Fred has been kidnapped, and now we're talking with robots? What explanation was going to cover this?

The Three Presidents

The silence was broken by Lincoln.
"Magic."

Chapter Five

"Magic. Right. That's the only thing that makes sense," I said. I stifled the impulse to roll my eyes because rolling my eyes at America's favorite president seemed disrespectful, even if he was really just a robot.

I could accept the idea of robot presidents who could talk and move around—I'd been to Disney World—but magic? Nope. I wasn't buying that.

"Speaking of magic," Lincoln said, "Our esteemed colleague Mr. Nixon found where our maker was secretly taping the premises. Please take advantage of this amazing modern technology and play the recording, good sir."

Before Nixon could get to the computer, Roosevelt had bounced back into the seat. "Allow me, my friends!" he said enthusiastically.

We crowded around him. I gently grabbed Liz and subtly moved her behind me. She had to stand on her tiptoes and lean to the side to see the screen, but I wanted to be between her and the three presidents. Whoever or whatever they were, these three seemed harmless enough, but—despite my interest in seeing what answers the security recording could provide about Fred—my first duty here was to protect my daughter.

I did not know what to make of these three guys, but I figured the playback was going to tell me something. Roosevelt, who handled the technology surprisingly well for a supposed recreation of a president from more than a century ago, pulled up the footage. He moved the recording to a spot where we could see Fred talking to his aide, Mr. Templeton, downstairs in the living room.

Fred, balding and soft-looking, despite being rather spry for his sixty-something years, towered over his assistant. Mr. Templeton was smaller and thinner. I always assumed the guy was a jogger or he biked a lot—he had that kind of build. I had been around Templeton a little, but we had never talked much.

I heard Fred's voice on the recording. "Barry, I'm sorry, but this isn't working. I think you need to go. We can't work together anymore. What you're wanting is just...not good. And your dumb ideas just slow me down anyway. I swear, if I could've found a chimpanzee with opposable thumbs, I would have fired you two months ago."

Fred ran a hand through what remained of his hair, giving himself a wispy Einstein look. "And I don't see how I can trust you anymore. Things are happening with the androids that don't make sense. And your bizarre blend of genuine insights and rookie mistakes are driving me crazy. I'm letting you go. No...I mean, yes, I'm firing you." He nodded his head vigorously, like he was having an internal dialogue over what to do, and he had just made up his mind.

Templeton pointed his finger at Fred and unloaded on him. "You arrogant, insufferable fool! You think I'm going to let you get in our way? You're wrong! Vicky and I have worked and planned too long for this."

Templeton ran to the front of the house. We watched in silence as he punched the security code and threw the door open. Four men rushed inside, passed Templeton, and headed toward Fred. The four intruders were dressed all in black. They were all big, intimidating, and mean-looking.

Fred tried to fight them, sort of, but he did not offer much resistance. Physicality was not something he was known for. He probably figured he would just get hurt worse if he caused too much trouble, and he would have been right.

21

"Barry, this won't work. I activated my contingency plan before you even showed up for work today. You know, because I'm smarter than you."

One of the four henchmen turned toward Templeton. "Contingency plan? You didn't say nuthin' about that. This is supposed to be a simple grab and go."

"It is," Templeton replied. "Take him—don't hurt him—and let's get out of here. Quickly!"

One of the men threw a blanket over Fred's head, and they rushed him out the door.

Roosevelt turned off the video.

It was vintage Fred—totally misreading an interpersonal dynamic and managing to be insufferably arrogant in the process. It always amazed me how he could go through each day without getting shot.

Was this why Fred wanted to hire me? He made it clear in that recording that he suspected trouble was coming. Did he want me to be his muscle?

Meanwhile, the three presidents were all staring at Liz, waiting for her response. I was still completely unimportant to them. But now that I had some idea of what the situation was, I could start to deal with it. I had enough information that I could formulate all the right questions.

Why was Fred taken?

Where was he now?

Who—or what—were these three guys?

Why was my daughter so important to them?

That last question was where we were going to start.

Chapter Six

I was content to let the authorities figure out the answers to most of my questions, but there was one matter I wanted to settle immediately. "We're calling the police so they can sort this out. Templeton made it clear that he doesn't want Fred hurt, so there's that. But before we bring in the cops, you've got about thirty seconds to explain why you three are so taken with my daughter."

Lincoln held up a soothing hand. "We can't do that."

"Oh, I'm pretty sure you can."

"He means we can't call the authorities," Nixon grumbled.

"But about my daughter..." I waved in the air, gesturing for them to talk. Taking care of Fred was only my second concern here.

As Nixon examined the tops of his shoes, Lincoln looked at Roosevelt and said, "Perhaps you should explain, Mr. President."

"Thank you, Mr. President," Roosevelt replied.

I sighed and rubbed my hand over my face impatiently.

"We were periodically brought to life, as it were, so that Dr. Perkins—"

"Wait. *Doctor* Perkins?"

"Yes," Roosevelt said. "The man has a doctorate."

"It's honorary," I replied, making no effort to keep the exasperation out of my voice.

Roosevelt stared at me as if waiting for some kind of point or further explanation. I offered him none.

"Okay, fine. Whatever. Just…talk," I said.

Roosevelt continued, "As I was saying, he would bring us to life, or activate us, I suppose you might say, to test our reflexes and responses."

"To gauge how normal—how human we were acting," said Nixon.

"Quite right. As Dr. Perkins became concerned about Mr. Templeton, the good doctor began to give us, eh, modern sensibilities. President Nixon was given a facility for utilizing cell phones, and I received some rudimentary computer skills. Dr. Perkins also gave us certain…"

He seemed to be groping for the right word, and Lincoln supplied it. "Priorities."

Liz looked as confused as I felt. "What kind of priorities?" I asked.

Roosevelt again took over the explanations. "We were told to prioritize the health and welfare of Dr. Perkins, his daughter Elaine, and the kids—Liz and Nolan. Dr. Perkins's latest information upload included that Mrs. Galloway was on a business trip and Nolan was away at college. We were told that if something happened to Dr. Perkins, and Elaine was out of town, we could trust Liz to help us rescue him, and in turn, we would protect her."

"What about my dad?" Liz asked.

Roosevelt looked at Nixon, who shrugged, then Roosevelt turned to Lincoln, who responded, "Well now, Liz, your grandfather was quite complimentary of your dad's fighting skills and…singing ability."

"Oh really?" My tone betrayed my skepticism.

"He was somewhat complimentary," Lincoln said.

I raised an eyebrow.

"It was a one-sentence reference in a much larger upload of information. But the main point here is that he acknowledged that you could be useful and had talent, so don't go giving yourself a case of the hypo."

"He thinks you're a wild card," Nixon said.

"Oh."

"He thinks you're unpredictable, which makes you unreliable," Nixon added.

"I get it," I said.

"He thinks you're okay if there's some rough stuff, but he looks at you as being hard to count on because of what you went through in the military and some of your other choices."

"I said 'I get it!'"

Everybody kind of froze and stared at me. Great. Fred implied I was unstable, and I responded by losing my temper.

Leave it to Fred to drive me crazy without even being in the room. That thought caused me a fresh wave of irritation—I was blaming Fred because I lost my temper.

The man had a rare talent for bringing out the worst in me.

I shook my head to clear my thoughts. I needed to focus on what was happening to Fred right now, and I needed to stay vigilant regarding the three weirdos.

"Can—can you prove that you're androids?" Liz asked, which was just about the most sensible question in the world at that point.

Interestingly, the other two seemed to look to Roosevelt for guidance. Then, the Rough Rider turned his head to the left without moving the rest of his body. His head twisted a little too far for a human neck to manage, which was both creepy and gross. He reached up with his right hand, rubbed his index finger against his neck, and a flap of skin peeled open, revealing a bunch of circuitry inside.

Simultaneously, I said, "Eww," as Liz said, "Cool!"

"All right, now that I have seen the strangest thing I am going to see today, I guess it's time to call 5-0," I said.

"What is 5-0?" Roosevelt asked.

"He is making reference to the local constabulary—the police department," Lincoln said.

"Wait, how did you know that?" Liz asked. She turned to me as if I would have an explanation for how a recreation from the 1800s would understand a TV reference.

"While President Roosevelt was given a mastery of computers, and President Nixon gained a working knowledge of cellular technology, I have been given an understanding of modern language," Lincoln said.

"That's cool, I guess," said Liz.

"Indeed! I am quite pleased with the gift Dr. Perkins bestowed upon me." Lincoln turned to me and said, "I used the term 'priorities' a little bit ago. Did you know that the plural of 'priority' was not a word during my lifetime? The thinking was that you could only have one priority, so to pluralize the term seemed self-contradictory. I find that interesting. Do you think that is interesting?"

An honest question deserved an honest reply from me. "No. No, I didn't know that, and no, I do not find it interesting."

"Dad," Liz said. That one word carried a rebuke. She was not pleased with my attitude.

"Anyway," I said, changing the subject—or more accurately—getting us back to the subject at hand, "we need to call the police."

"We can't do that," Nixon sounded irritated. "Templeton told Dr. Perkins that if we could be perfected—flawless examples of real people—then there was a gold mine there. Anyone in the world could be replaced with an android. How much money would criminals or foreign enemies pay for that? Dr. Perkins realized he was right, and then he realized he couldn't trust anyone. Who wouldn't be tempted by that kind of payoff?"

"Huh," I said. "Imagine a Richard Nixon robot being paranoid." But even as I said it, I knew this was not about

26

Nixon's feelings or programming or whatever. Fred didn't know who to trust. Despite our differences, I had to concede that he had been shrewd about this.

"Even paranoids have enemies," Nixon replied, which reminded me that this used to be a saying I heard when I was a kid.

"The point being," Roosevelt said, "We do not feel comfortable contacting the police. We three presidents cannot be discovered. We do not know who we can trust—outside of Liz, her brother, and her mother."

"It is up to us—the three presidents and Liz—to go and rescue Dr. Perkins. But you are welcome to accompany us, Mr. Galloway," said Lincoln.

"Thank you ever so much," I said with a slight bow. "How kind of you. But my daughter is not going anywhere except home. I'll take her there, then I'll go with you. If you don't want the police, fine."

"What if they send someone to your house to grab the girl to use as leverage over Dr. Perkins?" Nixon asked.

I found him quite annoying, but he had a point. I wanted to argue it, but I couldn't. The only way I could help Fred was to go with them—this was a big and lucrative secret, and they were right—I didn't know who we could trust locally. And I couldn't leave Liz at home by herself because I couldn't protect her there. I could drop her off at a friend's house, but what if we were being surveilled? That sounded paranoid in my mind, but these robots could be huge money. Bad guys would not be reluctant to invest major cash into stealing this kind of tech.

"All right, fine. Liz stays with us for now, but how are we supposed to find Fred? Any bright ideas?"

Roosevelt frowned.

Lincoln rubbed his beard-covered chin.

"I have one." Nixon's eyes narrowed at me as he spoke. "But I don't think you're going to like it."

Chapter Seven

"President Roosevelt was the police commissioner of New York City for a while," Nixon said.

"Police commissioner? Like, in Batman?" Liz asked.

"Yeah, like Batman," Nixon replied. He seemed a little annoyed by the question. I guess he didn't appreciate being interrupted.

"Who is Batman?" Lincoln asked Roosevelt, who shrugged.

"My point is," Nixon began, sounding exasperated at Lincoln's question, "Theodore has actually been involved in fighting crime and apprehending criminals, so he should be in charge."

"Huh uh, nope, I'm not taking directions from a robot." I couldn't help but consider that a crazy idea.

"Android," the three presidents said simultaneously.

"Whatever," I said, trying to not let their unison answer weird me out.

"To be fair, Theodore is the most logical choice, Mr. Galloway." Lincoln was in full country lawyer mode—friend of all, enemy of none, but still working an angle.

"Come on, Dad."

This was not a battle I was prepared to fight. Primarily because I wasn't sure what to do to find Fred. "Fine. Sure. Okay, Commissioner Roosevelt, whatcha got?"

Roosevelt took off his glasses and began to clean them with a handkerchief. The other two presidents and Liz were mesmerized by him. It looked like he was stalling, but if he was a robot, shouldn't his computer brain have instantly calculated a course of action or concluded that it had insufficient data or something? Or were his computer processes slowed down to go at whatever speed it would take the real Roosevelt to think up a solution?

I shook my head at the absurdity of it all. *Fred, what have you done?*

Roosevelt put his handkerchief away. "I do my best thinking while walking. After me." And with that, he marched right out the door.

The other two presidents grinned at each other and scrambled to catch up with him.

"Come on, Dad! Last one in the hall is a Nolan Galloway!"

Roosevelt marched the length of the hallway, down the stairs, and in a circle in Fred's big living room. Fred's tastes ran to oversized chairs and couches and a gigantic TV hanging on the wall. The place reeked of nerdy bachelor chic. He had moved here to be closer to Elaine and the kids after his latest trophy wife left him, and the interior decorating clearly lacked a woman's sensibilities.

The Bull Moose President did three circuits around the living room, power walking all the way with the rest of us dutifully following in his wake. He then took us back up the stairs and into the room where Liz and I had first met him.

I couldn't take it anymore. "This is ridiculous."

Roosevelt held up a triumphant finger and sported an equally triumphant grin, which was only partially obscured by his oversized moustache. "I have a plan."

"Okay, maybe I could have been more patient." The presidents ignored me, but at least Liz grinned.

"We will go to the house of this Templeton fellow," Roosevelt said.

"You think he's dumb enough to kidnap his boss and take him home?" I was not impressed with Roosevelt's robot programming at that moment.

"No," Roosevelt frowned at me. "I think we should look through Templeton's papers and possessions to see if we can find any clues regarding his whereabouts, his assets, and/or his agenda."

"That...sounds like a better-than-terrible first step," I conceded. Maybe it was time to stop being so condescending toward the robots.

Nixon clapped his hands and nodded his head vigorously. He reminded me of one of those toy windup apes that nods and claps cymbals together. I smirked at the thought, but if anyone noticed my expression, they didn't care.

"Great! We have a plan," Nixon said. "Does anyone know where Templeton lives?"

"I don't suppose there's a map around here," Lincoln said. "I've had a little experience as a surveyor, so if I could get myself a handle on the lay of the land, it might give us a bit of a perspective on things."

I frowned. Pulling up a map of the city on my phone was not a problem, but figuring out Templeton's whereabouts would be. Our needle was in a bigger haystack than Lincoln could imagine. Templeton had put some planning into Fred's kidnapping, so I didn't know how easy it would be to pull Templeton's address from the internet. The man had probably made an effort to cover his tracks.

"I know where he lives!" Liz was literally bouncing on her feet, excited about being the person with the answer in a conversation with her military dad and three faux presidents. "Mom and Nolan and me went to his house last December, Dad. We went to a Christmas party there when you were...in Nashville."

Liz had paused because her exuberance was spoiled by her obvious memory of me and the Nashville trip. It had not gone well. My big career leap from the Navy to my next big thing had ended with a whimper in Nashville, and it was right before Christmas.

Ho ho ho.

"Well? Where does Templeton live, girl?" Nixon asked.

She smiled at Nixon, more polite than warm, then looked at me. "Cardinal Lane. I remember, Dad, because I had never heard of that street before, and the Cardinals are your favorite baseball team, and I talked to Mom and Nolan about how you were missing out on a chance to be on Cardinal Lane. We can use the GPS to get to the street, and then I can get us to the house. It's really big and really isolated. We won't be able to miss it."

The five of us moved to walk out of the room again. This time, we had a plan of attack. Cool.

"So you say it's a big house? It's funny that an assistant to a tightwad toymaker would have a big house." That seemed a little off to me.

"Maybe he married into money," Roosevelt suggested.

"Or perhaps Dr. Perkins is a more generous employer than you give him credit for," Lincoln said.

I started to offer a rebuttal to Lincoln, but Liz side-eyed me, so I shut my mouth and walked.

As we filed down the stairs, Liz grabbed my wrist to slow me down. After allowing some distance to develop between us and the three presidents, Liz spoke softly. "I don't get it."

I shook my head, showing her that I didn't know what she was referring to.

"I understand why Grandpa would make a Lincoln— everybody loves Lincoln." She was leaning in and whispering to me as we walked. "And Roosevelt is cool. You can tell he's a lot of fun. But why would Grandpa make an android Richard Nixon? I mean, Watergate? Hello? I mean," she said again, "I don't know what Watergate was, but it was bad, right?" She shook her head at the absurdity of Nixon's presence.

We had reached the bottom of the stairs where our path was blocked by the object of our discussion. And he did not look happy. It was clear that his robot ears worked better than Liz gave them credit for.

"Well, I guess your grandfather figured he needed to create someone who knew how to drive a modern car, so 'hello' yourself." Nixon stalked off toward the kitchen. His anger was impossible to miss.

Liz's eyes were huge. "Oh, Daddy! I'm so embarrassed."

"It's okay."

"But I feel *so* bad! I'm like, one of those mean girls or something."

"Nixon's just a cranky, chippy dude. If it wasn't this, it would be something else." I spoke extra softly. I wanted her to feel better, but I didn't want him to be mad at me too.

Liz looked like she was about to cry. Lincoln came over and put a hand on her shoulder. "Liz, dear, it's okay. Sometimes hard questions have to be asked, and the real answers are not so comfortable. Let's just focus on rescuing Dr. Perkins."

As if on cue, Roosevelt emerged from the kitchen, pumping both fists in the air in triumph, followed by the stoop-shouldered Nixon. "President Nixon found the car keys where Dr. Perkins so helpfully left them hanging—by the door going into the garage. All right, Richard, we will rely on you as we attempt to go find a lead about our maker."

Roosevelt continued to pump his fists and turned back toward the kitchen. Nixon literally beamed in response to Roosevelt's appreciative words. I guess even robots have heroes.

Once we exited the kitchen, I hit the switch to open the garage door, and then we all climbed into Fred's

Explorer. Nixon and I sat up front with Roosevelt and Lincoln behind us and Liz in the rear.

"What is this GPS you referred to earlier, Miss Liz?" Lincoln asked.

I hit the button on the remote to close the garage as we departed. "Take a right as you exit," I said to Nixon.

Handing Lincoln my phone, I answered for Liz, "GPS is something we can pull up on our phones to help us with directions. You can see the map there that will take us to Cardinal Lane."

"What an extraordinary invention! What a wonder! Oh, Richard, take a left at the end of the block."

Lincoln took over giving Nixon directions for the next twenty-five minutes or so. Nixon turned out to be a good driver. I mean, the real Nixon would have driven a lot in his life, so on the one hand, it wasn't that big a deal. But this wasn't the real Nixon, it was a robot, so I was impressed by how well he could drive. I had to admit—in the privacy of my thoughts—that Fred really was kind of brilliant.

Nixon smoothly merged into traffic on Pellissippi Parkway and drove for several miles before exiting and heading east. It was early enough in the day that the traffic in Knoxville wasn't that bad yet.

The sixteenth president guided his colleague through several more turns before saying, "Okay, Richard, a road will appear on your right in three quarters of a mile. Take it, and we will be on Cardinal Lane."

Lincoln went back to marveling over our modern technology, then started reminiscing. "You know, Liz, I was a bit of an inventor myself back in the days of yore."

I was only half-listening. I was thinking about what we might find at Templeton's place. I expected the man to be somewhere far away, and he'd probably removed anything incriminating that he could think of, but maybe we would find a lead. I was a firm believer that doing something was better than doing nothing.

My vision issues were also a bit of a distraction. I was squinting behind my prescription sunglasses because the clouds had gone, and it had gotten sunny. I prayed that my eyes would recover sooner rather than later.

Lincoln was still prattling on about an award he had gotten for something. I probably would have understood it if I had cared what he was talking about, but I didn't. "And the thing about my patent was," said Lincoln, before he was interrupted by a loud cracking sound, "Oh! Oh my goodness!"

Chapter Eight

"You broke my phone!"

Lincoln had pried the protective case off my device, and now my phone was in two pieces that he cradled in his big hands

"Mr. Galloway, I am profoundly sorry, I was just trying to get a look inside, and…here we are. Maybe I can fix it. Please don't go and give yourself a case of the hypo over this."

"You keep saying 'a case of the hypo,' like anybody in this car has a single idea what you're talking about! And…you broke my phone, which is…really inconvenient."

Nixon shot me a look. "You need to calm down."

That comment, of course, left me even more irritated. I took a big breath so I could tell both Lincoln and Nixon what I thought about them when Liz chimed in. "I recognize where we are! If you keep going, it'll be—I don't know—maybe about a half mile down the road on the left. There's a super long driveway."

I gently rapped the side of my fist against my window. I was irritated about the phone, but really, I was aggravated about this situation. We couldn't go to the cops—I guess. I could accept that for the time being—though I did suddenly wonder if I would be in trouble with the law for failure to report a crime. I felt confident about protecting myself on the off chance that someone was at Templeton's house waiting for us. I had my martial arts ability and a gun.

but my bar was set much higher for protecting Liz. I was 95% sure I could keep myself safe, but that percentage wasn't high enough when it came to her safety.

Maybe I needed to pull the plug on this operation. If Lincoln was right, and a person could truly only have one priority, well, my priority was not Fred Perkins; it was Liz. I could make an anonymous call and let the cops investigate Templeton. The three robot presidents could storm the Bastille, go back and hide at Fred's place, or head for the hills. I didn't care.

I smacked my car window again—this time hard enough that Liz gasped. I had taken an oath to defend my country. The three presidents were right: the technology they represented was a gamechanger that posed a threat to national security. Anyone could be replaced by a robot if it was of the quality of these three in the car. I needed to do something to stop this before it got out of hand. Since I wasn't sure who to trust, I couldn't call the cops.

It wasn't about Fred. It was about America. That sounded a little *Zippity Doo Dah*, I knew that, but it was the truth. The stakes were, potentially, incredibly high.

I could contact people I trusted in the Navy, but they couldn't operate on American soil without politicians getting involved. Who could I trust? I didn't know, but I could at least do some recon, gather some intel.

This might be the dumbest thing I ever did—I'm sure Elaine would think so—but I figured a dumb plan was better than no plan at all. I stole a glance at Liz and prayed that God would keep her safe, even if I was too stupid to do that myself.

"We're here," said Nixon.

"Excellent driving, Richard! Good man!" Roosevelt had lost none of his enthusiasm during the drive.

"Now what?" asked Nixon.

"Go straight up the driveway and brake at the last second," Roosevelt said without hesitation. "Liz, dear? Put your head down and don't look up unless I say it's okay."

As Nixon drove the length of the long driveway, I breathed another prayer.

Nixon slammed on the brakes dangerously close to Templeton's four-car garage. I had never seen a garage that big before, but that wasn't remotely interesting to me at the moment. I was about to jump out of the vehicle when I was stopped short by the sound of a question.

"Why is Templeton's garage so big?" Clearly, Nixon found this issue more interesting than I did.

"What?" Liz started to look up.

I snapped my head around fast enough to see her starting to expose herself to danger. "Down!" I hissed at her.

She jerked her head low.

"Who cares about the guy's garage?" I asked, but it was almost as much a statement as it was a question.

"We should care," said Lincoln. "How could a man on an assistant's salary afford such fancy accommodations? While I raised the possibility that Dr. Perkins paid well, I would not think Mr. Templeton's house would be nicer than Dr. Perkins.'"

"Precisely," Roosevelt chimed in. "There's outside money involved here unless, as I said before, Mr. Templeton married into it. Good question, Richard. And, again, excellent driving."

I swear Nixon started blushing.

This little chat was getting us nowhere. "You guys can ask Templeton all the questions you want after I liberate Fred. I mean, on the extremely remote chance he's in there."

"In case someone is here, we'll form a barrier in front of Liz as we advance," said Roosevelt. "We'll create a three-man line. I'll take the center, a step and a half in front of you two," he said to his fellow presidents. Abraham, you'll be on my right side. Richard, you'll take the left. Mr. Galloway will go before us because he is the most expendable."

Roosevelt looked directly at me. "I apologize for my bluntness, sir, but we are pressed for time, I think. And of course, there's probably no one here anyway. I'm reasonably confident that this will be completely safe."

He smiled.

I didn't.

It was not lost on me that any advantage we had from zipping up the driveway was lost by the chatty presidents wasting time talking about the garage and how to walk to the front door. But there was probably no one here anyway—that's what we kept telling ourselves. We were just going to go inside and search for clues that might indicate Fred's whereabouts.

Better safe than sorry though. I jumped out of the car, pulled my gun, and pointed it at the ground. I hunched my shoulders a little and scrambled to the front door.

The house was enormous—three stories tall and as wide as maybe four normal houses. But, yeah, let's focus on the garage size.

I was saddled with amateurs.

There were four steps leading up to the porch. I took them two at a time. Despite almost hurting myself on Fred's front door just a little while ago, I decided to kick the door open to gain entry into Templeton's house.

As I prepared to launch my right foot, something unexpected happened.

Chapter Nine

Templeton's front door opened, and a woman stepped outside. "Hi, Liz!" The woman's face beamed when she saw my daughter. "It is so nice to see you again!"

The woman was petite—smaller than Templeton—and she was wearing blue overalls with a white tee shirt and an oversized hat. The small bucket and spade in her hands completed the look of a person who was about to throw herself into a little gardening.

Her eyes widened as she took in the rest of us. "You—some of you men seem familiar, but I am terrible with names. My word, you look just like Abraham Lincoln! Even your clothes look like his. I bet you hear that all the time." She laughed good-naturedly.

The woman shook her head as if clearing her thoughts. "What are you all doing here? Do you have a meeting with my husband?"

"Why as a matter of fact we do," said Lincoln. "And we're running late. Would you mind letting us in to see him right away? Just point the way." Lincoln joined me on the porch.

I had slipped my gun out of her line of sight when I judged her not to be a threat. She gave no indication that she had noticed it.

Mrs. Templeton's smile deepened. "That would be just fine. Come on in and head off to the right. Down the hall, you'll come to his library."

"You guys go on ahead," I said to the three presidents. "Liz and I will just wait in the car." I'm not sure why I said that. It was just a gut impulse. But I trusted my gut.

Liz started to protest, but I cut her off with a curt shake of my head. I smiled at Templeton's wife. "Really, it's just my three friends who had the meeting with your husband. They're actors—community theater, which is why they're dressed up. Liz and I were just along for the ride."

Mrs. Templeton frowned at me as if she was deep in thought. "You two might want to join your friends."

"Why?" My question was pointed, as was my tone, but I didn't care.

She smiled sadly. "Barry came home this morning unexpectedly. I don't know why he isn't at work, but all I could get out of him was 'They just left me behind.' I don't know what that means, but he acted really upset. I don't know who 'they' are. I don't think Fred has hired any more employees. It seems like a business thing, maybe a side job. If a business opportunity fell through, maybe a more positive meeting will perk him up. And I know seeing Liz will make him happy. Barry has always liked Fred's grandkids."

"Come on, Dad. Let's go cheer up Mr. Templeton while we can," Liz said.

"Yeah, Galloway, don't be a party pooper," Nixon added as he walked by me.

So Templeton was here, but Fred wasn't? Maybe I did need to go in and see him. I could question him before the trail got cold.

Mrs. Templeton held the door for us as we entered the house. The living room was humongous, which was unsurprising. There were elevator doors to our left, a hallway that disappeared around a corner on our right, and a balcony over the far side of the room that served as a hallway for the second floor. It made Fred's oversized living room look like a closet.

40

"You said the library is to the right, correct?" Roosevelt asked as he headed in that direction in his typical bold manner.

"Why don't you just hold on a minute there, Teddy?"

We all whirled around at the sound of Mrs. Templeton's voice. Her tone had shifted from the sweet, southern gardener vibe. She was standing in the elevator, holding the door open with one hand and with her phone in the other. "Barry dear, I just solved all your problems. I've got the three presidents, the granddaughter, and the half-blind son-in-law in the living room." She paused and listened to her husband's response before frowning. "Of course, I sealed the front door behind me. They're fish in a barrel. Now, come out and gloat."

"You're not very ladylike," Lincoln said to Mrs. Templeton.

She replied with a gesture involving both hands that really just served to underscore Lincoln's point, then she let the elevator door close.

"Mr. Galloway, would you mind checking the most direct route of egress?" Roosevelt requested. I was impressed with how calm he sounded.

I grabbed Liz by the hand, and as I turned around, I saw that while the door looked like wood when standing on the porch, from the inside point of view it was solid metal. It was clearly even more unforgiving than Fred's front door. There was a keypad next to the doorknob. I tried to turn the knob, but as I expected, it did not budge.

At that point I heard Barry Templeton's voice from on high. He was standing on the balcony. "Galloway, I saw your weapon when I was watching y'all arrive. Surveillance cameras are a wonderful thing. Take your gun, release the clip, remove the bullet from the chamber, dismantle the weapon, and throw everything on the floor."

He crossed his arms like some Roman emperor. I didn't appreciate the smug expression on his face, so I decided to do something about it.

I pulled out my weapon and pointed it at him in one smooth move. "How about instead I just shoot you, tear this place apart until I find Fred, and—just to make this memorable—burn your house to the ground on our way out the door?"

He smiled. "Fred said you liked to make jokes."

I smiled back. But I kept the gun aimed at him.

"He doesn't think you're very funny," Templeton added.

"Everyone's a critic. But that's enough snappy banter. Tell me where he is, and maybe I'll spare you the house-burning and the bullet hole."

My weak eyes were locked in on the balcony until I heard movement in front of me. Simultaneous to the sound, I heard Roosevelt softly say, "Mr. Galloway, you might want to consider the new friends who've come to our party."

I spared a quick glance and saw four tough-looking guys—probably the same ones who had grabbed Fred. They had quietly slipped in from around a corner and were standing under the balcony. The men were dressed in black jumpsuits with Kevlar vests.

The four of them were aiming guns at us. I'd had guns pointed at me before, and I never enjoyed the experience, but this time was the worst.

This time my daughter was in the room.

Chapter Ten

"We're all going to stay calm," I said. "Liz, my three friends, and I are all just going to leave. You can keep Fred. I don't care."

"Dad!" said Liz.

"Not now, Honey," I replied.

"That really would be unacceptable, Mr. Galloway," said Roosevelt.

"Yes, it would," Templeton agreed. "Lose the gun before my employees lose their patience."

I winced and took a few seconds, trying desperately to think of an alternative to putting down my piece. Nothing came to mind. With an angry sigh, I did everything Templeton had told me to do, slowly unloading and dismantling the gun.

"Excellent! Now, take the girl and," Templeton paused, thinking it over, "Nixon. Take Nixon. Let the rest of them just sit here."

"We're not going with you, and you're not going to shoot us," said Nixon.

"What makes you say that?" asked one of the bad guys. He was tall and a little plump. He also sported a shaved head and an old scar under his left eye.

"That's actually a restaurant-quality question," I said.

"You probably only want Liz so you can get Dr. Perkins to do what you want, and you need the three of us because our technology is what this is all about, right?" Nixon said.

"I don't care about technology; I only care about the money I'm getting," said Scar Guy.

"Nixon's right," Templeton admitted. "However, we really don't need Galloway at all, so if you presidents act up, you risk losing him."

"You'll have to get past all of us to get to the girl," said Roosevelt.

"We'd rather protect the girl than Galloway, so," Nixon shrugged. When that earned him a frown from Lincoln, Nixon just shrugged again.

"I just don't even have words for this day anymore," I muttered.

"We will fight to protect Liz," Roosevelt reiterated.

"This is getting frustrating," Templeton said. "All right, boys, holster your guns. I don't even want you to shoot at Galloway. I wouldn't want the girl to catch a stray, and I don't want you to risk damaging the merchandise too badly."

"That's fine by me." Scar Guy put away his gun. "There's been too much talking already as far as I'm concerned. Time to do something about that."

He advanced toward me, as the rest of his team fanned out and moved toward the three presidents.

"I'll take the blind guy," he told his men, and then to me he said, "I heard you were in the Navy. Always hated you Squids. I served two and a half years in the Army before I got out. It wasn't violent enough for me." He had a wolfish grin. "It's been a while since I beat up a Squid."

"There are three things you should know," I said. "One, I'm not blind. Two, I don't get all caught up in the rivalries between the branches."

"And three?"

"Three: I've kind of dabbled in the martial arts. And by 'dabble' I mean I have multiple black belts."

"Is that supposed to impress me?" He put his fists up and assumed a stance that showed me he thought he knew how to box because he had watched other people fight.

"I was kind of hoping so," I said.

"Why? You too scared to fight?"

"No, I just try to avoid it when I can."

He made a noise indicating his disgust with me then took a swing. I blocked his punch, pulled him off balance, and before he knew it, he was on his back.

I spared a quick glance at the others, and they were a wonder to behold. Roosevelt jabbed his opponent with three quick lefts before landing a powerful right cross. Lincoln had his man in a headlock, and Nixon was holding his own, grappling with the last of our adversaries.

My opponent crab-walked away from me, moving on hands and feet with his back slightly off the ground, as he created distance between us. I was surprised he had so little fight in him.

"Fall back!" he ordered.

His men quickly complied. Nixon's adversary disengaged and retreated. Roosevelt's man was staggering, but he managed to stumble back the way he had come.

Lincoln released his guy from a headlock. The sixteenth president called after his retreating foe, "You have nothing to be ashamed of. You acquitted yourself well. You had no way of knowing what an experienced wrestler I was."

I was confused by how easy that was. As the presidents and I exchanged bewildered looks, I suddenly felt a surge of panic. I spun around 360 degrees.

"Liz!" I called out. But she was gone. It was crazy. There was no way someone could have gotten around us to grab her, and the front door had not opened or closed. Had she just vanished in thin air? Was there a trapdoor?

Whatever the explanation, Liz had been taken.

Chapter Eleven

My mouth hung open, and my breath came in ragged gasps. I felt a surge of fear over my daughter being taken, then my mind went someplace darker. There shouldn't be anything more terrible than having your daughter kidnapped, but for me—just for a moment—there was a paralyzing fear that was even greater.

In the privacy of my thoughts, my self-preservation instinct temporarily overwhelmed my fatherly concern for my child. It was shameful, but in that instant my past was too much for me to bear. In the moment, all I could think about was the time when I was the one who had been taken.

I was serving my country overseas when I was captured by the enemy. They tortured me, and my chest, back, and arms still bore the scars. I wanted, I *needed*, to shake off the memories and focus on the here and now—focus on Liz—but for a few seconds I couldn't. Just like I couldn't shake the memory of what I had done to escape my captivity.

"This is terrible—the absolute worst," Nixon said. I could barely hear the words, not because he spoke softly but because he was drowned out by a roaring sound. I guess my blood pressure was skyrocketing or something.

I was dimly aware of Lincoln trying to get Nixon to shut up.

The next thing I knew, Roosevelt grabbed me by the shoulders. My distress must have been obvious to him. I knocked his hands away, but he grabbed me again. "Pull it together, man!" he yelled in my face. "If you lose your composure, you won't do Liz any good. They won't hurt her. They'll just use her to get Dr. Perkins to do what they want."

That made sense. They wouldn't hurt her—at least not right away. Time was my ally. It took me a second to realize I had actually mumbled those words out loud. "Time is my ally." I said it again, louder this time, to Roosevelt, who nodded.

I said it a third time, calming myself down. I saw Templeton still standing on the balcony with that smug look on his face.

This was not a time for fear. And it certainly was not a time for a stroll down memory lane. I willed myself to not think about my captivity.

No, this was a time for action. Seeing Templeton up there with his stupid grin gave me the perfect idea for what that action should be.

The balcony he was on served as a hallway connecting one side of the second floor with the other. The balcony sported a wooden handrail that was roughly waist high on him, and the handrail was held up by wooden spindles.

I ran toward him, and his grin morphed into a confused expression. Without slowing down, I planted my right foot on the floor, high-stepped with my left onto a small table located against a wall, jumped up, and grabbed onto the base of the second floor. My hands landed between the spindles. I dangled there for less than a second. I shimmied up and over the railing faster than a monkey chasing a banana. By the time my feet touched the balcony floor I discovered Templeton had decided not to wait around to watch me.

He was running away as fast as he could. Strangely— if the word "strangely" could be applied to anything more today—there were two sets of elevator doors side by side, and he was headed straight for them. Why did the Templetons have two elevators next to each other in their three-story house? And why was there just one set of elevator doors on the first floor?

This was a day full of questions.

Templeton made it to the left-hand elevator, but I was going to catch him before the doors closed. He reached into his pocket, pulled his balled-up hand back out, and made a gesture of flinging whatever was inside at me. I slid to halt and brought my hands up to protect myself from…nothing.

His hand had been empty. He laughed as the elevator doors closed in front of me.

"Inventors," I said through gritted teeth.

I bent the middle finger of my right hand and used my knuckle to stab the button located between the elevators. It was a longstanding trait I had developed to avoid getting other people's germs on my fingertips. It's funny the little habits you hold onto, even as everything in your world is going insane.

Maybe holding onto our little habits is what keeps us from losing our minds when life gets crazy. But this wasn't the time to be philosophical. My brain was going all over the place, but I needed to focus. Had I been out of the game for too long? No, for Liz's sake, I was going to lock in and do what needed to be done.

As I waited, I worked through my options. The elevator to my right opened, and I jumped inside. Using my knuckle again, I punched the button for the third floor, ignoring all the other buttons on the panel.

Instead of taking me up one floor level, my elevator car lurched to a stop midway. There was a screen on the elevator wall that lit up just then. It was Templeton's wife. She was wearing a smug smile that was similar to her husband's.

I smiled back at her. "Oh, hey, hi! Ya know, I bet your involvement in this has just been a big misunderstanding. I mean, if you could tell me where my daughter is, and *maybe* give me a hint as to Fred's whereabouts, I bet the police wouldn't be interested in you at all."

"Really?" she smiled. "Is that the best you've got?"

I smiled more broadly. "Look, Lady Templeton—I'm sorry I don't remember your first name—I think maybe your husband has gotten a little, um, overzealous about something that I probably don't even care about. I just need to know where my daughter is."

"My name is Vicky, and I know exactly what you're doing."

"You do? That's interesting because I thought I was just kinda winging it."

She tilted her head slightly and began to play with her hair. Her smile had changed. It looked, I don't know, I guess kind of coy or something. "You're trying to dazzle me with your smile and your witty charm," she said. "And don't get me started on that hair. But I'm not falling for it. Not for any of it." She waved her free hand—the one that wasn't in her hair—in a circle in front of her, palm out, as if she was encompassing everything about me and rejecting it. "My family has wanted something for generations, and thanks to Fred Perkins, their dream is going to become my reality. Mine and Barry's."

I scanned the elevator car, desperate for a way out. "I promise I'm not flirting with you; I'm a happily married man. I'm also a father. Speaking of which, where's my daughter?" My voice had an edge to it. I needed to know Liz was safe.

She replied with an impatient frown. "Don't worry about your daughter—she's fine. We're not going to harm a feather on the golden goose."

"I'll be the judge of what's fine where she is concerned. Now where is she?"

"That's the wrong question," Vicky Templeton said.

"I can't think of anything in the world that would be more important for me to ask."

Her smile turned hard and ugly. "No? Well, try this one: How long can you hold your breath?"

She turned her gaze to something offscreen. She reached over and hit a switch, then I heard the unmistakable hissing sound of gas being released into the elevator car.

Chapter Twelve

I only gradually became aware that I was conscious. I was laying on something hard, probably a floor. There was a light on, which I could tell without opening my eyes. I reached up to see if my stupid glasses were on. I didn't want to open my eyes and find myself looking directly at a light source. Ah, I had my glasses. Praise the Lord for small victories.

My head hurt a little, but I could ignore that.

Then I heard a sound. It was an unpleasant noise that grated on my nerves. A voice. It was a sound that was not nearly as easy to ignore as my headache.

Fred's voice.

"Hey? Are you finally awake? Good. You're not going to go crazy on me are you? I mean, because you're in captivity again. It's not going to make you go berserk, right?"

"Hello, Fred." I punctuated my greeting with an unnaturally long sigh.

"Yeah, hi. What are you doing here?"

I sat up and very carefully began to open my eyes. "Isn't it obvious? I'm rescuing you. How're we doing so far?"

He started to respond, but I interrupted him. "Give me a minute, will you? I need to get the lay of the land."

Fred was sitting on a cot that had sheets, a blanket, and a pillow, so it was clear that they weren't planning to treat him too badly. There was a tray next to him with a half-eaten meal on it. I sat up from my spot on the floor. We were surrounded by bars—a singular prison cell. Outside of our cage there was a long table that was roughly thirty feet away from us. The table had two chairs and two computers. The table was unmanned. Fred and I were alone.

I took it all in, but I didn't say anything when I was done. I just wasn't super enthusiastic about talking to Fred.

Apparently, the elongated silence was too much for him. "Well, how about it?"

"How about what?" I asked.

"How'd you get here? Do you have a plan to get out? Are you going to have flashbacks to being a prisoner?"

"Stop asking me that."

"I'm sorry," he said, but he sounded more perturbed than sorry. "I just imagine it was rough before, and now you're back in the same situation."

"This is not remotely the same situation," I replied. And I hoped my current scenario stayed different from the last one.

"Why do you say that?" Fred persisted.

"Because I don't see a car battery with wires attached to it, nor do I see a man holding a knife over an open flame," I snapped. I walked over to the cell door, grabbed the bars, and rattled them to test how sturdy they were. Okay, that wasn't true. I yanked on the bars because I wanted to work off some steam.

It didn't help.

"I'm sorry," Fred said.

That surprised me. He sounded sincere. Sympathy was not something I had ever associated with Fred.

"I guess prison can change a man," I mumbled, then smiled at my own joke.

"What?"

"Huh?"

"Never mind. What are you doing here?" he asked.

"Your three favorite presidents tricked Liz and I into going to your place, we discovered you were kidnapped, came here, and got ambushed."

"What? How did—how are the presidents doing? I mean, are they functioning well? Are they believable?"

"I would think you would be more concerned about your granddaughter." I was a little disgusted with Fred.

"Sure, yeah, um, how are the four of them?"

"Liz was taken from us after we got to the house."

"Oh, no. Yeah, Barry said he might bring her in to give me some incentive to play ball. He wants me to build replacements for world leaders and CEOs. Big money there. But, yeah, she'll be fine. I mean she'll be fine for now. If I tell him 'no' again then…I don't know. Threats might be made."

I wanted to snap at him for being so cavalier about her safety, but I had to tell myself that she was okay—I couldn't let my imagination go anywhere else on the subject—and I forced myself to move on. I could be really good at compartmentalizing.

Besides, Vicky had said they weren't going to hurt Liz, and Vicky had no incentive to lie; she had known her knockout gas was about to do its magic.

I had to move on to something else. "Were you tempted at all? Did the money tempt you?" I was genuinely curious.

He shrugged it off. "Liz and Nolan's grandmother was a saint—God rest her soul—but I have three ex-wives, so I'm never getting rich. Why earn dirty money just to hand most of it over to them?"

"That's…a beautiful testament to integrity," I said.

A silence stretched between us that he ended up breaking.

"So, do you have a plan?"

"Well," I began slowly, "If we could figure out how to get out of this cell—"

"Oh, I can get us out of the cell," Fred almost sneered—like breaking out of here was nothing.

"If you could get out, then why didn't you?"

"Because then I would have to navigate through five levels of subbasement to get to the first floor of Templeton's house, and then I'd have to get past all his goons."

"Good point," I conceded. "So this cell is located under the house? That's good to know. But how, exactly, can you get out here?"

Fred frowned at me. "All those times I told you I was a genius—did you think I was kidding?"

I massaged my temples and closed my eyes. "I should have just stayed at home, Fred. I swear, after a 48-hour, nonstop dose of your ego, the Templetons would have begged us to take you back."

Chapter Thirteen

"There are things you should know before I get us out of the cell," Fred said.

"Like what?" I was ready to go find Liz, but if Fred had useful intel, I knew I needed to make myself be patient and listen to it, even if I didn't want to.

As he talked, I rattled the cell bars again. It occurred to me that I probably did this as a subconscious effort to not be trapped in a small space with Fred. Maybe the Templetons were more adept at torture than I had given them credit for.

"The Templetons want to take advantage of my brilliance, but they have different motivations. Barry wants to figure out the tech so he can make a lot of money on it. I just wanted to make the presidents for an amusement park or something; he figured out that my androids could be so good that they could replace world leaders, entrepreneurs, movie stars—whoever had money. Kidnappers would buy the androids, so a rich person could be taken, and no one would be looking for them because their android replacements would be so perfect."

"That makes sense," I said, choosing to ignore Fred's casual mention of his 'brilliance.'"

He got off his cot and began to pace in the confined space. He tended to get animated when he had something he could say that he knew and you didn't. "The wife, um, uh," he snapped his fingers, "Margaret—"

"Vicky," I corrected.

"Really? Are you sure? Huh, I thought it was Margaret."

"Yes, it's Vicky. Move it along please."

"Fine. Anyway, she's a Nazi."

I kicked the bars. "Oh, come on, Fred. Calling someone a Nazi because you don't like her politics is so overdone."

"No, you don't get it. She's an actual, literal Nazi."

"What?" I shook my head. That little bombshell was…unexpected.

"Her great grandfather was a Nazi scientist, you know, like from World War Two."

"Okay, you don't get to insult me. I've heard of Nazis; you don't have to explain to me where they're from," I said.

"Sure. Fine," Fred shook his head and waved a hand in the air dismissively. "The great grandfather came to Knoxville after the war and got this house. For the last eighty years, the family has been building and expanding and turning the place into a lab, a fortress, a kind of maze, and who knows what else. She explained it all to me."

"Why, exactly, would she walk you through all that?

"She and her husband both tried to persuade me to join their cause—or causes, since they have different agendas. She was actually just talking to me when she got the call that one of their cameras spotted you turning onto their street. She was in the middle of telling me that history is written by the winners, and the Nazis got some bad PR. She said they have some really good ideas when you give them a chance."

"So? Did she persuade you?"

"Hah hah. You're so funny. Yeah, she persuaded me. I've always been open minded when it comes to Nazis. That's why I'm still in the cell," said Fred.

"Anything else you need to tell me before we make our dramatic exit? They aren't going to leave us alone forever," I pointed out.

"There's a control room with video feeds that's one floor up. We should probably go there first, but it'll be tricky because, like I said, there's a bit of a maze."

"Yeah, about that, what do you mean by 'a maze'?"

Fred looked confused. "I'm not sure how to explain that in simpler terms. It's a maaaze." He drew the word out.

I rolled my eyes. "Did you walk through the maze? Could you retrace your steps? Did they give you a grand tour on the way to the dungeon here?"

"They sort of did. They were all buddy-buddy. They really want me to agree to work with them, and they wanted me to understand how sophisticated and well-organized they are. But I don't know the exact way back through the maze."

"That's disappointing."

"I'm sorry. Despite how much they sugarcoated it, I was still in the process of being abducted. It didn't occur to me to leave a trail of breadcrumbs."

"Take it easy. I'm just glad they didn't turn you into a Nazi in the few hours they had with you," I said. I was ready for him to wrap things up. I looked impatiently out to the door on the other side of the room, silently praying that no one would walk through it.

"I wasn't remotely tempted. When it comes to my work, I don't like to collaborate—other people just slow me down. That's why Templeton was my assistant instead of my partner, but he even screwed that up."

Then Fred added, "And I'm not a Nazi."

"Thanks for adding that last part," I said. "So, if they're trying so hard to woo you, why did they show up at your place with four thugs?"

"Their plan was to steal a couple of the presidents and see if they could figure out the technology and programming on their own, but when I fired Templeton, he chose to improvise and grab me. They were going to go ahead and take some androids too, but I told him I had contingency plans, so they got nervous, just took me, and ran."

"Makes sense, I guess. We'd better get out of here."

Fred walked over to the cell door. The locking mechanism faced away from us. It was easy to reach, but hard to see. Fred reached through the bars and began to grope for the keypad blindly.

"You know the combination?" I asked.

"A guard brought me food, and I watched his hand movements. It might take me a couple of tries, but I can figure it out."

I made a noise. I had started to say something, but I didn't know exactly what.

His fingers continued to move. "It's okay to say you're impressed."

"To be honest, I actually am impressed. Very observant of you, Fred."

I heard a click, and our cell door was unlocked.

"Good! Let's go," I said. "Let's find Liz and get out of here."

Just then, the door across the room opened.

A guard walked in.

He did not seem happy.

He did seem armed.

Chapter Fourteen

"Stand down!" I barked at the guard, pointing my finger at his face for emphasis and walking toward him.

He rested a hand on his holstered gun. "Stop right there, shut up, and get back in the cell. I'm not afraid of your finger."

I turned slightly, executed an angled somersault through the air, and raked my foot across his forehead before I landed. He dropped to one knee, and I unleashed a right-left combo, Wing Chun-style, and knocked him out.

"You really just can't help but show off, can you?" Fred was clearly not impressed. Well, it might be more accurate to say he was trying to act like he wasn't impressed, but somersaults are cool. Everybody knows that.

I took the unconscious man's gun and cell phone off him, grabbed him under his armpits, and began to drag him to the cell.

"Fine. I'll let you knock out the next bad guy," I said.

"No, I'll stay in my lane," Fred replied.

I dropped the guard in the cell and turned my attention to his phone, which I could not access. For a second, I considered waking the guy up and compelling him to unlock it, but I literally shook my head at the thought. I would not—I could not—torture another human being. Instead, I threw his phone on the floor as hard as I could.

As pieces of the cell phone flew in five different directions, Fred—clearly irritated—said, "Hey! I could have hacked that."

"Oh. Sorry." I was frustrated with myself, but I hid it from him as best I could.

"Man! You're like a bull in a China shop."

I ignored him and headed for the door the bad guy had used to enter the room. I heard Fred scurrying behind me to catch up.

As I opened the door, I took a quick step back instead of going into the hall. Fred collided with me, then he apologized too loudly. I glared at him, which of course prompted another apology that was, again, too loud.

"You are terrible at escapes," I hissed at him.

"Sorry!" He hunched over and then whispered, "sorry" again, as if lowering his stature would lower his volume.

I exhaled as I mumbled, "Civilians."

I took a quick peek into the hall, checking left and right, before moving out and gesturing for Fred to follow me. There was nothing about the hallway that felt like it was part of the basement of a house. It gave off more of a military or industrial complex kind of vibe. It was definitely part of something bigger than a normal house. The hallway might have stretched the length of a football field, and it had all kinds of doors on both sides. What was on the other side of those doors—more cells, security offices, supplies for if the facility was under siege? I had no idea. I was roughly twenty feet from one end of the hall—at which there was door that hopefully led to a stairway up to the main house—when it suddenly hit me that Liz might be behind one of these doors we were about to rush by.

I stifled the impulse to swear. Why wasn't my thinking sharper? It had been a while since I had been on an op, and I had also been hit by some kind of knockout gas. It was tempting to blame Fred because he was a distraction, but that would have been childish and weak of me. Was I distracted by worry over Liz? No, I truly believed that she was in no immediate danger if the Templetons were wanting to use her to force Fred to work with them.

Was I damaged goods because I had been taken prisoner once before? No, that might be how I would phrase it if I was discussing it with someone else, but I knew how I should word the question if I was ready to be honest: Was I damaged goods because of what I had to do to escape that previous captivity?

No, that still wasn't right. Was I damaged goods because of what I chose to do to escape?

Yep, that was the right question. But this was not the time to think about it.

"Sooo are we just going to stand here and hope for the best?"

God help me! I didn't even realize that I was just standing still in the middle of the hallway. Pushing aside all other thoughts, I said, "No. Let's move."

It was at that point that we heard the footsteps. I didn't realize it, but at the end of the hall, right before the doors that led to wherever, there was a side hallway, and I could hear the echo of footsteps coming our way.

Chapter Fifteen

I grabbed Fred by the collar with one hand, then lurched toward the nearest door. I pulled it open and saw a huge storage room. Jerking Fred inside, I closed the door and locked it. I had to lock it by feel because the room was pitch black.

"How'd you know this room was empty?"

"I didn't."

"But then why—"

"I'm an optimist, now be quiet," I hissed.

After a few seconds, my eyes had not adjusted at all. I was still standing in total darkness. I had led Fred into a blackhole. I couldn't move because there was zero visibility.

With a sigh of disgust, I pulled my sunglasses off and crammed them into my pocket. Things would go a lot easier if I wasn't an idiot. Immediately, I began to make out various shapes and objects.

Now we could move.

I used both hands to grab Fred by the head so I could find his ear and whisper into it. "Listen: You're going to quietly and gently slip through here to the back of the room—as far from the door as possible."

Shockingly, Fred began moving without having to talk about it first. We felt our way along at a snail's pace, easing around some objects and pushing others out of our way. When we got to the back of the room, we discovered that there was an area off to the side that was around the corner. After we got as far away from the door as possible, we could almost talk at normal levels without fear of being overheard by anyone in the hall.

"We'll wait a minute, then try to leave. When they discover that we've escaped, they might go door to door, but hopefully they don't think we're dumb enough to lock ourselves in a storage room on purpose," I said.

"That's your plan--to do something so stupid that they won't expect it?"

"Pretty bold, huh?"

"That's not the word I would use, but if we're going to be stuck for a minute, you need to actually answer the question I keep asking."

"What question is that?" I figured as long as I was going to act dumb, I might as well commit to the part.

"How do I know that you're not going to flake out?" he asked.

"'Cause I told you I wouldn't."

"That's not good enough."

"It'll have to do because that's all you're getting," I said.

"No, I'm counting on you, and so is Liz, and so are the three presidents. I need to know you're going to be reliable."

"I don't know how I can convince you of that," I said. I was uncomfortable with this. It was probably time for us to move.

As if on cue, I heard yelling out in the hall. When that stopped, I heard someone rattling our locked door. Surely, the guard had keys. When the door did not immediately open, I wondered if maybe every guard did not have every key. Would they call for the Keeper of the Keys and then go door to door, checking every room? I once again chose to hope that they would not think we would lock ourselves in a room.

There was more yelling then silence. I was not sure if they were waiting outside our door, or if they had moved on.

"We'll wait for a bit," I said.

"Good. You have time to tell me what happened to you when you got captured."

I had never come so close to punching Fred in the face as I was in that moment. But I restrained myself.

Fred had no right to ask me such a personal question. It was none of his business. But then I decided I was going to tell him anyway. It wasn't that he deserved an answer. It really wasn't about him at all.

In that split second, I decided I needed to do this for me. The time had come. I needed to talk about my time as a prisoner.

Chapter Sixteen

I had told Elaine what happened to me on my last stint overseas, and I had written my report for the Navy, but that was it. I had never spoken of these things with any friends or another family member or a professional. I mean, I had gone through the motions with mandatory counseling, but I didn't really unpack what happened, and the counselor quickly figured out that I wasn't a threat to myself or anyone else, so he signed off on me.

It felt weird that Fred was the one I was going to talk to about it now. I mean, technically, he was family, but the guy had the people skills of Hepatitis B.

Did Fred have a right to know what had happened? No, but I hadn't talked about this in months, and it still weighed on me.

A lot.

"All right, listen up because I don't want to repeat myself. You knew I got captured."

"Yeah." Fred was wiping his hands up and down on his pants. I figured he had a lot of nervous sweat going on despite the coolness of the air-conditioned room.

"They worked me over pretty good for three days on and off." That was an incredible understatement, but it was easier to speak glibly about it and move on rather than think about what they put me through.

"But you got out."

"Yeah, I got out. This young woman—probably a teenager, maybe not older than Liz—she brought me food."

I took a couple of deep breaths. My feelings were all in a jumble. I didn't *want* to talk about this. I should have been over by the door, listening for the guards in the hall and preparing to make a move. But I *needed* to talk about it, and I was going to be worthless until I did. I'm not sure why these feelings were suddenly so overwhelming, but they were.

"So? What happened?" Fred wasn't super patient even under ideal conditions, and these conditions were far from ideal.

"The girl brought me a fork with one of my meals. She hadn't done that before, not even when the cuisine called for it. I bent back one of the tines on the fork and used it to pick the lock on the cuffs they had on me, and I made my escape. The girl gave me the tool to get myself free, and she did it on purpose."

I stopped talking. The seconds stretched by in the darkness.

"That was, um, a pretty vanilla escape story. I expected, I don't know, something more," Fred said.

I grimaced and silently and repeatedly bumped the side of my fist against the wall. "That's because that's not the whole story." I paused and took some more deep breaths. "When they originally brought me in, I walked by a room with an open door. The room was full of incendiaries. On my way out, I rigged up an explosive device big enough to take down the whole house. And it did."

"I guess that covered your escape," Fred said.

"Yeah, and then some. It created an inferno. I'm sure everyone inside…didn't make it. I guess…I figure there was a decent chance the girl was inside the house. I…probably killed her. Don't you see? She saved my life, and that's how I repaid her."

"I bet you felt guilty," Fred said, and it was obvious to me that he wasn't trying to be mean, he was just that lacking in social skills.

"Yeah, you could say I felt guilty. So, I got out of the Service—which you complained about, even though you complained when I went in and then again every time I re-upped."

"I was always against it because it was hard on Elaine and the kids, but you were getting close to getting your full retirement, so it surprised me when you came home."

I wasn't interested in being lectured to about how my choices affected Elaine by a guy who'd had four wives.

"Don't interrupt me; I'm on a roll. I got out, but I had my next thing lined up, so it didn't matter, right? A Christian music exec liked my demo tape, so I went down to Nashville to cross my T's and dot my I's, and then it blew up." I rolled my eyes at the unfortunate pun.

Fred snickered, then coughed softly to cover up his laughter.

I ignored it and pressed on. "They kept asking me what my message was. 'What did I want to say?' 'What was going to make me stand out among other artists?'"

"And what was it?" Fred asked. "What big, special thing did you have to say?"

"That was the problem. I didn't want to *say* anything, at least not anything that was going on inside me. I couldn't stop thinking about the girl. There I was, the star-spangled Navy boy, fresh out of the Service, a war hero who was going to sing for Jesus. But I didn't want to open up because I was afraid I would say something about the girl. And my guilt over possibly killing her."

I winced at the memory of it. "And that is one of the harder parts of the whole thing. I don't know that she's dead. I don't know that she was injured at all. She might have been. Maybe she probably was…I just don't know."

I paused, but Fred had nothing to say.

"And the more I didn't talk about it, the more guilt I felt." I punctuated my sentence with a long, slow sigh. It was like letting the air out of a balloon full of shame or something.

"So, you tanked two careers because the girl *might* have been in the house, and she *might* have died in the explosion?"

"That's one way to look at it," I was back to being irritated by Fred.

"I've got one question," Fred said. My bad eyes had adjusted well enough in the dark room to see that the guy was raising his hand like a student in a classroom.

"What?" My tone was as uninviting as I could possibly make it.

"What happened to the fork?"

Chapter Seventeen

"I have no idea what happened to the fork." I had to enunciate slowly to keep myself from losing my cool and yelling at the guy. "I imagine it was blown to smithereens."

"Then you didn't take it with you, right?"

"I don't re—" But all of a sudden, I did remember. I didn't know why something so stupid mattered, but I figured answering the question was easier than talking about how dumb it was.

"The fork got stuck in the lock, so I left it. I remember because I wanted to use the fork as a weapon, but I needed to get out of there, so I left it behind. Satisfied?"

"Yes."

I could hear smugness in Fred's voice, which in and of itself was not unusual. Fred could roll out of bed on three hours' sleep and do a TED Talk on what it's like to be smug.

But like a moth to a flame, I couldn't resist asking why he was smug about this conversation. "Who cares about the fork?"

"Don't you see?" he asked.

He shook his head, like he was baffled at my cluelessness.

"Clearly, I don't." I was getting impatient. It was past time to move. And talking had not made me feel better.

"If you hadn't set off the bomb, the bad guys would have found the fork, and they would have figured out that the girl had ruined their plans for you." He paused. "They

69

would have killed her, right? You setting off that bomb might have saved her. It was the only chance she had."

He chuckled, which did not really fit the conversation, but that was Fred. "Really, she only did for you what you did for her. She didn't rescue you; she just gave you a fork. There was no guarantee you could pick a lock with it. There was also no way of knowing if you would be able to escape. She just gave you a chance to maybe survive. When you blew up the evidence of her helping you, it did not guarantee that things would work out for her, but you gave her a chance to get away with it. You both made choices that put your lives in danger, you both gave each other a chance to live. I'd say you were about as even as you could possibly be."

I sagged backward against the wall and slowly sank to the floor. My mouth hung open in shock. I had been carrying this for months—almost a year really. And the answer was right there the whole time. Peace of mind was right in front of me. Hours and hours of obsessive thoughts and prayers, and all it took was a conversation with Fred (of all people)!

I wanted to laugh and cry and throw up—all at the same time.

"See? It pays to talk to a genius," Fred said.

Okay, that snapped me out of it. "Time to move," I replied. I got up and began threading my way through the room to get back to the door and into the hallway. I felt more alive than I had since before my captivity. It was time to find Liz and the three presidents and go home.

Chapter Eighteen

As we moved through the storage room, Fred banged into three different things. I shushed him but only after the first two times of listening to him both apologize and complain too loudly.

I would process my gratitude later. For now, I just needed him to be quiet.

When I reached the door, I groped around until one hand found the lock. I fished my special glasses out of my pocket and put them on. I had a fleeting thought about giving Fred instructions before throwing the door open and leaping into the hall, but I figured that would be pointless. He earned my respect for his insight regarding the girl who helped me, but that didn't mean I thought he would suddenly be able to handle any rough stuff.

After taking two deep breaths, I unlocked the door and threw it open. There was a single guard located about fifteen feet from my position. I plowed forward and drove him into the opposite wall. He grunted but offered little resistance before I flipped him to the ground and knocked him out.

He was wearing a suit and tie, not a uniform. I checked inside his jacket, the small of his back, and his ankles, looking for a weapon. I had already taken a gun from the last guard I knocked out, but I figured that two guns were better than one.

"Hmm, no gun, just a set of Filipino fighting sticks—I can work with that."

"No gun. Right," Fred said. "See? They really don't want to hurt me or Liz or anybody else."

"Yeah," I replied. "These Nazis sure are nice people when you give them a chance and keep an open mind."

"You don't have to be sarcastic."

I pursed my lips to cut off the reply I was about to make.

"Do you think you could teach me that Kung Fu stuff?" Fred asked as he moved from the doorway into the hall.

I gave him a thorough look of appraisal. "No."

"Hey! You don't have to be so blunt."

I was already gliding down the hall on the balls of my feet, heading toward the stairway. I spared him a quick backward glance to make sure he was following. "I'm kidding," I said, and I meant it. Mostly.

Keeping one of the fighting sticks for myself, I handed Fred the other one. I had little faith that he could do anything constructive with it, but I wanted to keep my gun hand free, so I could only use one of the sticks anyway.

I stopped at the doors that led to the stairwell. When Fred caught up with me, I plunged through.

"What's the plan?" Fred blurted out, once again being too loud.

Standing in the stairway, I whirled around on him, got in his face, and whispered, "We're going to go up to the next floor and check out the surveillance room you mentioned. And we're going to do it without talking. If there'd been someone on the stairs, you would have alerted them to our presence."

"I'm sorry," he whispered back. "This is my first jailbreak."

"It's going to be your last if you keep screwing up."

"I said I was sorry," he murmured, but I was moving up the stairs and didn't bother replying.

When I got to the double doors one level up, I spied through the glass a guard standing watch. I had the gun in my waistband, and the fighting stick in my left hand. Without hesitation, I opened the door. As the guard began to turn toward me, I grabbed him with my free hand, hooked him with the fighting stick, and pulled him into the stairwell.

This time, my opponent put up a good fight. Twice, he almost pushed me down the stairs, he even got my stick away from me, but ultimately, I put a chokehold on him until he was unconscious.

As I started to enter the hall, Fred said, "You're pretty rough with these guys."

"I haven't killed anyone. Yet. Now, if you could go at least thirty seconds without offering commentary, our chances of not getting caught would probably improve."

"You're so testy," Fred sounded irritated.

"If you're not enjoying my company, you could always go back to your cell."

"I'll...make the best of it."

I pushed open the doors into the hallway, at which point I realized that in fact there was no hallway. The window had been hard to see through, and the guard's head had blocked most of my field of vision. Now that I was out on this floor, I saw that instead of an open hallway, there was a wall in front of me with three doors in it.

I opened the door on the right and told Fred I would be back in two seconds. Ignoring his protest at being left alone, I walked through the doorway. One second later, I came back to Fred through the middle door.

"That seems like a waste of a maze-space," I observed.

"Don't scare me like that. We need to stick together."

He was right, but I had no intention of telling him that.

"We should take the door on the left," he said.

"You realize that it comes across as condescending when you tell people obvious things, right? I mean, there are three doors, and the first two don't lead anywhere, so yeah, we need to take the door on the left. Do you go out of your way to irritate people on purpose?"

Fred put his hand on the doorknob but stretched back as far as he could from it. Clearly, he was wanting me to go through it first, which was fine. I was much better equipped for whatever was on the other side.

"What can I say? Almost everything is obvious to me. If I didn't state the obvious, I practically wouldn't talk at all."

He opened the door and stepped back.

I took a couple of quick steps into whatever was beyond the door. As it turned out, there was no one on the other side, which was nice.

"Hmm, maybe should consider that approach for a while—you practically not talking at all."

"Hardy har har. What do you see?"

"Check it out for yourself." As Fred followed me into the new area, we found ourselves in a cramped space with brick walls—we hadn't seen brick walls before—and steps leading up a level to a small landing and another door.

"We probably don't want to go up another level. The room with the surveillance cameras is on this floor," he said.

"I was kind of counting on you to have some idea of how to get us where we need to go. You're the one who got the tour." I gestured at the stairs. "If we don't go up there, where do we go?"

Fred began meandering around the tiny space. "I don't know."

"But they showed it to you!"

"I'm sorry! It was my first abduction. I had a lot on my mind."

I rubbed my chin with my fighting stick. I didn't have an itch; I just needed some kind of movement. "I'd have been better off if I was stuck with Nixon."

"Hey!" Fred stopped pacing and looked at me. His tone shifted from offended to curious as he asked, "So honestly, how was Nixon? Was he kind of grating on your nerves? I wanted him to be kind of grating."

"He was adorable. Let's go." I started up the stairs.

"But we don't want to go up a level," Fred said. He followed me anyway.

"No, we don't, but Liz isn't here, so we keep moving."

We got to the top of the stairs and stopped in front of the door. It was painted a vivid blue, which was unlike any of the colors of any of the other doors. Why were there brick walls and a blue door here? I had no idea. The door had a handle instead of knob. Why was it all different? It didn't really matter to me, but then I had a stray thought that maybe it was supposed to matter. Maybe it helped the bad guys navigate the maze.

This wasn't the time to try and solve riddles that might not be riddles, though; it was time to cover ground and find my daughter.

I pressed down on the handle and stepped forward as the door opened.

"Jesus!" I yelled, but I wasn't swearing. I was praying. There was no floor on the other side of the door, and I barely stopped myself from falling. I was supporting myself with my right foot on solid flooring and my left hand holding onto the door handle. If I had been moving just a little faster or stopped a half second slower, I would have dropped like a stone.

Before I could pull myself back, though, Fred plowed into me from behind. He grunted and stopped where he was. I was not so fortunate.

Chapter Nineteen

"Ah! I'm sorry! I've always been kind of clumsy. Hey, don't let go! PE was the worst back in high school. I hated all those sports. Just no coordination at all. It's like every good gene I had went to my brain—none to my coordination. You probably can't relate to any of that."

Fred continued to prattle on as I hung over the abyss. The only light I had was that which was coming from the area where Fred was still standing.

I had kept one hand on the door handle after he bumped me over the edge. The door swung out—and so of course it swung me out. I dropped my fighting stick, which I had been holding in the hand that wasn't gripping the door. The only thing I had to fight at that moment was gravity. I grabbed onto the handle with my free hand as the door continued to move.

Looking back from where I had come, I saw that there were rungs attached to the wall underneath the door frame. I waited as the door slowly swung me back to where I had started. When I was close enough, I reached out and grabbed the top rung. I let go of the door and began climbing down the wall. When my feet touched the floor, lights came on.

I picked up my fighting stick and began to reconnoiter the area.

"Hey, don't get too far ahead of me," Fred said. "Wait down there."

"Don't fall on me," I grumbled.

Fred moved gingerly down the rungs and stood beside me. As he was descending, I was scanning our surroundings. We were standing in an open area with three hallways threading out in front of us like spokes on a wheel. I started down the one on the left because why not? We walked roughly one hundred feet before coming up to a wall. I tapped it in a couple of places with my stick, shrugged at Fred, then headed back the way we came.

"This is tedious," Fred complained.

"You can always go back and wait in the cell." I had already made that offer to him, but I thought it was worth repeating.

"No, that's okay. I'll stick it out."

We arrived back at the opening where the three hallways met. I glanced up and saw that the door I had entered through was still hanging open. I was thankful I didn't fall and break a leg when Fred bumped into me.

It was time to pick a second option for our route out of here. I skipped the hallway in the middle and went to the far one because, again, why not?

We quickly arrived at another wall. I tapped it with my fighting stick, as much from irritation and nervous energy as anything else, and then, much to my great surprise, one of my taps made a funny sound.

Fred and I stared at each other. "I think you found a door or something," he said.

Using my hand that carried the fighting stick, I pushed the spot that made the funny noise, and the wall gave way. I raised my gun as I waited to see what was on the other side.

I thought it might open into a cramped, secret passageway, or a regular hallway, but it turned out to be a normal looking room. There was a table with six computer monitors on it and seating for two people. This was the surveillance room Fred had told me about. There was an exit on the far side, so at least this wasn't a dead end, which was good news.

The most immediate concern I had, though, was that there was a man in the room. He was slightly overweight with pasty skin and red hair. He was standing up, several feet from the table with the monitors. He had been helping himself to a drink from a coffee station. The actual part of this that was the most concerning was that the man was looking at us, and he acted totally unruffled. He wasn't rushing to call for help or pulling out a weapon. He was just standing there with his coffee in hand. And he was smiling.

Why was he smiling?

Chapter Twenty

"Well, well, well, look what the cat dragged in," said the surveillance guy.

"Are you always so casual when your captives break out?" I asked, genuinely curious. His attitude was all the more surprising given that I was pointing a gun at him.

He chuckled. "You're not really *my* captives. I'm not the one who's going to get in trouble for you breaking out, and it's not a big deal anyway."

He gestured toward the coffee station with his cup. "Would you like some coffee? We have a nice selection of flavors and plenty of sugar and cream."

"Do you have any decaf?" Fred asked. "Caffeine makes me jittery. I can barely drink sodas." He stared at the coffee station with genuine longing in his eyes.

"We're not drinking Nazi coffee," I said, using my best command tone from my years in the Navy.

"I'm not a Nazi," said the guy.

"Yeah, whatever it takes to help you sleep at night." I pointed at the computer monitors. "But I don't care about your politics. I need you to get over there and find my daughter."

He shrugged. "Sure. Why not."

My eyes narrowed. Why was he so accommodating? His quick compliance caused me to change plans. "Fred, do you think you can operate that system?" I pointed at the work area.

"Does a perpendicular bisector intersect a line at a 90 degree angle?" he replied.

"How would I know! Why don't you just answer me like a normal person?"

"Sorry. Yes."

The surveillance guy grinned. "You guys are funny. I'm sure Perkins can do it, but I can do it quicker, and I don't care. It's not a big deal to me if you see where your daughter is. Whichever room she's in right now, she's doing fine."

My gaze shifted back and forth from the Templeton's henchman to Fred. I decided that faster was better, and I motioned with my gun for the guy to get to work.

He slowly walked across the room, cradling his coffee cup in his hands. His decision to use both hands to hold the cup was interesting in that it would make it more difficult for him to pull out a weapon—if he was so inclined—unless he wanted to use his hot coffee to attack me.

His shirt was tucked into his pants, and his pants were tucked into his boots. As he crossed in front of me and I saw his back, it was clear that he did not have quick access to any weapon on his person. He might be concealing something in a pocket, but he came across as non-threatening.

As he seated himself at his workstation, he said, "You know the only reason you're out and about is the Templetons don't care. They can let you run around a little bit and stay busy. Perkins can see more of the facility. It just doesn't matter. Everyone and everything they want is either downstairs here or up in the mansion. All the dominoes are falling. You might as well agree to help them now, Perkins. The sooner you get on board, the sooner we all start getting rich."

"Pipe down and find my daughter," I said.

"Yeah, sure, keep your pants on."

He began switching feeds and showing us different locations upstairs, downstairs, and outside the house.

An alarm beeped and a red light lit up on a control panel.

"What's that?" Fred asked in an agitated voice.

"I'm getting summoned." The man reached for a button, but I dropped the fighting stick from my left hand and grabbed his wrist. "Ow, that hurts," he cried out.

"It'll hurt a lot worse when I break it. Don't touch anything without my permission." I would never torture a man, but I would hurt somebody in the line of duty if the situation necessitated it.

"I need to answer that. It'll be a one-way video feed. They won't see you."

"How do we know we can trust you?" asked Fred.

"I'm just an employee here, man. I just want to do techy stuff and get paid; I don't want a broken wrist."

He looked up at me, and I replied with a curt nod. I let go of him.

He hit a few switches and one of the monitors showed Vicky Templeton sitting in a study. She looked directly into the camera and said, "Be sure and record all of this, Sid."

"It's like she's staring right at us," Fred said.

"She's just looking at the camera. She can't see you," Sid said.

He hit two switches. "She'll see a light blink on her end. It's how she knows I'm recording. I could open a comm channel, but I assume you wouldn't like that."

I ignored him and watched in silence as her door opened. Two of her guards walked in, and they were not alone.

"Nixon," Fred said under his breath.

"Your androids are cool," Sid said.

"What do you want with me?" We heard Nixon say over the monitor.

"Won't you have a seat, Mr. President?" Vicky smiled and gestured to the chair located in front of the desk she was sitting behind.

He scowled at one guard, then the other. He paused as if thinking about taking them on but then plopped into the seat with a thud.

"What do you want?" he said again.

"I want you," she began, then she smiled bigger and tilted her head slightly to one side, "to join the team that will appreciate all that you offer. I want you to join us."

Chapter Twenty-One

"Oh no," murmured Fred.

For as anxious as I was to check on Liz, I reminded myself that she was in no immediate danger, as long as they were trying to win Fred over. In the meantime, this discussion between Vicky Templeton and Richard Nixon struck me as too important to miss.

"Do you mind if I call you 'Richard'?" she asked.

"I would prefer 'Mr. President' or 'Sir,' if it's all the same to you."

Her face tightened a little, but she held her smile. "We both know that you'll never really be accepted by the other presidents. Lincoln and Roosevelt—I bet they have quite the little lovefest going on. You'll never be treated like you're on equal footing with them."

"Where are they now?" Nixon asked. I wasn't sure if he expected an actual answer to that, or if he was just trying to redirect an insulting conversation. He was rubbing his hands together and squirming in his seat. If anybody wanted to watch someone who epitomized being uncomfortable in their own skin, I would tell them to download this.

"Last I heard, they were in the backyard." Vicky threw her hands up, "But it's a big backyard—trees and bushes and ditches—my people will get them, but I don't know how quickly."

"Sounds like you've got a mess on your hands," Nixon said. He smirked a little.

"Don't worry about me." Vicky's smile deepened. "We'll take care of business. But speaking of that, you could be a big help to us, and my husband and I would appreciate it."

Nixon looked confused, and he seemed frustrated by his confusion. "What are you talking about? You've got me. I'm your prisoner. What could you possibly want from me?"

"If you think you're being held captive, then you are misreading the situation. You're not a prisoner at all."

There was a pause as Nixon processed that little piece of intel with his robot brain. He finally said, "I'm free to go then." He stood up. "Fine. I'm leaving. I'll just check on Dr. Perkins and Liz, and we'll all be on our way."

"I'm so proud of him." Fred was beaming.

On the screen, I saw Vicky's two goons—who had been standing back near the door—each take two steps toward Nixon as he arose from his seat.

Vicky held up a hand, and they stopped in their tracks. But when she spoke, her words were aimed at Nixon. "Just a minute. Dr. Perkins is downstairs, thoroughly engrossed in his work. And you know how he gets when he is in the throes of creating magic."

"She's lying," Fred murmured.

I gave him an irritated look. "No kidding. Pipe down."

Vicky was still talking. "Liz is being interviewed by my husband. We're just trying to figure out the best way to incorporate her gifts into our work."

"If Dr. Perkins is on board with everything, then why are you trying to sweet talk me?"

"We want to conduct some tests and get your reactions, Mr. President. We can learn so much from you. We want to replicate your greatness, but to really understand how your, um, brain works, we want you to respond honestly to a variety of questions and stimuli. Your cooperation will make the work go faster. And rather than having Dr. Perkins order you to help us, we would prefer that you choose to help us on your own. We respect you that much. We want to be friends."

"Fine. Let me talk to Dr. Perkins—alone—and also Liz, and we can get started."

"I told you they were busy, and we don't want to waste a minute's time.

"You're a liar."

I sighed. Nixon's total lack of people skills was going to get him killed, if that was the right word for a robot who was inviting his captor's wrath.

Vicky's face reminded me of a volcano that was about to explode, but then I watched her calm herself. It seemed to tax her greatly, but she did it. Her hands were squeezing indentions into the arms of her chair, but she maintained her composure. When she finally spoke, she said, "Dr. Perkins will always like the other two presidents better. And they will always be closer to each other than they are to you. My husband and I are offering you friendship, and I know that you have been created," she groped for the right words, "authentically enough to want that. Let us be your friends. But you need to be our friend too. Help us."

"Come on, just make Richard do the right thing," whispered Fred.

"Tell me you did not just pray about a robot's life choices."

"He's an android," Sid the tech guy said.

I stifled my impulse to put a bullet through the computer monitor.

"Sometimes," Richard said, "it's not about friendship."

"Then what do you want? Money?" Vicky asked.

"What would I do with money?" Nixon acted disgusted by the notion. "It's not like I can go buy a house and live a normal life."

"Then...what?" Vicky looked at the two guards, as if they could explain it to her.

"It's about loyalty," Nixon was more passionate than I had seen him before. "It's about being able to count on people and them counting on you. That's what I want from the others, and that's what I'm going to give them. I don't believe that Dr. Perkins or Liz are helping you, and I am sticking with them. I don't care what you offer me."

"That's what Watergate was really all about. Loyalty. There were men who were loyal to Nixon, and—" Fred was gushing.

"Stop," I interrupted him. "This is not the time for a Watergate lecture. When that time comes, I will let you know. But...it's...probably never going to come."

Before Fred could reply to that, Vicky was talking again. "Fine. Have it your way. Boys," Vicky turned her attention to the guards. "Take the president to Lab Three. Make sure he's nice and comfortable."

The guards grabbed Nixon by the arms. He struggled, but it was in vain.

"Either the other two presidents or Galloway will rescue me."

"No, they won't. We'll take you apart piece by piece, and by then we will have captured your fellow androids. Galloway is already neutralized. Your precious Dr. Perkins can watch what we do to you, and if that doesn't get him to help us, maybe we'll use sweet little Liz to change his mind."

As the guards began to pull Nixon out of the room, he shouted, "Leave the girl alone! Do you hear me? We'll stop you! I swear it!"

When Nixon was out of the room, and the door was closed, Vicky looked at the camera again. "All right, Sid, edit out the part where we threatened the girl. I don't want Perkins to get all verklempt if by some fluke he came across this video. He's got the personality of cabbage, but the man is undeniably brilliant. And sneaky. If anybody could access this file, it would probably be him."

I turned to Fred and said softly, "Why do I feel like I'm listening to your next ex-wife?"

"Shut up." Fred said.

Sid turned to me. "I need to respond, or there will be a problem."

I pointed my gun at his head. "Say whatever you feel comfortable saying."

He swallowed, nodded, then reached for the communications control. "Okay, Mrs. Templeton, will do. Any other instructions?"

She looked up at the camera in her office and smiled. She really had a knack for turning the charm on and off on a dime. "Yes, give me an update on the two maze rats. Where are they?"

"They're, um, uh. Let me see. Yeah, they're nearby."

"Sounds good. Go ahead and have the men scoop them up and stick them back in their cell. We've been patient enough with Perkins. It's time to play some hardball."

Chapter Twenty-Two

Sid ended his call with Vicky and swiveled his chair around to face us. He held his hands out to his sides in a "What can I do?" gesture.

He started to speak, but I cut him off. Pointing at one of his monitors, I said, "Find my daughter."

"You're putting me in an awkward position. I didn't mind helping you because, like I said, it didn't matter. But now it does. Honestly, man, I'm afraid of Vicky. She is way scarier than Barry. If she wants you locked back up, I don't want to say no."

"Just let me do it," Fred said. "I can find Liz."

He sounded irritated, which—to be honest—kind of made me happy.

He pushed past Sid and started working the keyboard.

Sid got a pained expression on his face. "Come on, guys. This is a tough spot for me."

"Quiet," I said without much energy behind it. I had determined that Sid was not a threat, and now he wasn't a help, so I was kind of bored with him at this point.

Fred was scrolling through security feeds like he had been doing it his whole life. It was nice to be at a point in our odyssey where he was actually bringing something to the table. Ever since he got us out of our cell, he had pretty much just been a liability when it came to trying to find Liz and get out of here.

"There she is!" he exclaimed.

We were looking at a room that was quite similar to the one Vicky and Nixon had been in. There was a desk with a chair behind it and a bookcase behind that. In front of the desk there was a chair that faced it. Liz was seated, facing the desk. She was alone.

"Let me talk to her."

"It's a different channel than the one I used to talk to Vicky," said Sid.

"Give him the frequency," I said with as much menace as I could muster. I could never torture another person. I probably wouldn't have done it before, but certainly after what I had experienced, I just couldn't do it.

That said, I needed to talk to my daughter. I was sweating, and I could feel my heartbeat speeding up. How could I say that there was one line I would never cross, if I also said I would do anything to save my daughter? God help me, I did not know how to figure out the math on this.

The moment passed, as I saw onscreen the door to the office open and Barry Templeton walk in, escorted by two guards who stationed themselves by the door.

The coward—he needed two men to keep him safe from my sixteen-year-old daughter. Well, he was a smart coward. I had taught her enough that he would have needed help if she attacked him. Liz's problem—and at a time like this, it really was a problem—was not her skill level; it was her sweet spirit. She might not be ruthless enough to inflict the damage she would need to, if push came to shove.

"I'm very sorry I had to make you wait. I had been running some computer simulations, and I needed to read the data. I keep hoping that I can make a breakthrough that will make me less dependent on your grandfather. I would be happy to work with him of course, but sometimes, well, he's not the easiest guy, is he?" Barry punctuated his question with a smile. His smile reminded me of the way his wife smiled, which was weird.

Liz didn't say a word.

Barry even mimicked the way his wife tilted her head. It was almost like they were brother and sister, but I figured it was actually just that they isolated themselves from other people. Maybe they were alone together so much that they had picked up each other's mannerisms. I guess it's hard to find other couple friends who are greedy Nazis.

89

Barry let the silence linger a bit, then said, "Liz, Honey, we need your help with your grandfather."

"Please don't call me 'Honey,' sir." Liz's back was ramrod straight. She was making it clear that she was uncomfortable.

"You don't need to be standoffish, Liz. You are totally safe with me."

"If you hurt me, my dad will hurt you so bad. I've seen him break boards a bunch of times. One time, I saw him break, like, a concrete block. Imagine how hard he could hit your face."

I had never heard Liz talk like that in her entire life. She was normally sweet, but at this moment she sounded cold and mean. I was proud and inspired and terrified, all in equal measures.

"Can you really break a concrete block?" Sid asked.

"Quiet," said Fred.

Clearly, my father-in-law was not interested in a prolonged conversation about my martial arts abilities.

Barry slapped a hand down on the desktop. Liz jumped back against her chair, scooting it a few inches in the process.

"We don't have to make this tense between us," Barry said. "I'm not threatening you, and you don't have to threaten me. And your dad is not in a position to threaten anybody."

"I respectfully disagree," Sid murmured, but of course, Barry couldn't hear him.

"I want you to help us get your grandfather to work with us. I had wanted to take a few of the androids and conduct some experiments and do our own research, but his stupid contingency plans got in the way. Now, we've got him, and we've got you, so let's make this work, shall we?"

He paused, but Liz had nothing to say, so he pressed on. "What you need to be asking yourself is what *you* want.

I would love to see a win-win scenario here: we get something, you get something."

"My dad and the three presidents will rescue me, or Grandpa will rescue me. I'm not going to help you."

Barry shook his head. "Your dad, your grandfather, and Nixon are already locked up. We'll get those other two presidents any minute. Stop acting like a spoiled brat, and just…give us what we want. Name your price."

Liz jumped out of her seat, "Why don't you name *your* price? Is it thirty pieces of silver since you betrayed Grandpa?"

Barry arose from his chair to match her. He yelled at his guards, "Get her out of my sight!"

Chapter Twenty-Three

"Come on," I said to Fred. "Time to go get my daughter."

"We don't know where she is," he protested.

"I don't care. We'll open every door if we have to. But first, I need to take care of Sid."

Sid put his hands out in front of him and picked his feet up off the floor, as if making himself smaller would make him safer. "Don't kill me, man! I helped you."

"I'm not going to kill you. However, I am going to knock you out. Can't have you calling the cavalry on us. Now brace yourself. This is going to hurt you a lot more than it's going to hurt me."

Fred got between us and put his hands on my chest.

I frowned at him. "If you're working your nerve up to give me a hug, now is not a good time."

"What? Whatever. Listen: Don't knock Steve out."

"M-my name is Sid."

Fred looked confused. "Really? Are you sure? I thought it was Steve, but I'm terrible with names. No, hey, see Adam, we don't know our way through the maze, but I bet Steve does."

Fred smiled in triumph as he read the grudging acceptance on my face. "See? It keeps paying dividends to have a genius on the team," he said.

"Guys, come on. I didn't mind helping you, but I don't see how I can guide you around. That sounds like it would be big trouble for me."

"Oh, yeah? Maybe we should shoot you, if you don't want to help," Fred said.

I think he was trying for a menacing tone, but he didn't quite nail it. Liz was much scarier than he was.

"Where did that come from?" I asked. "You turned on a dime from 'Don't knock him out' to 'Hey, we could shoot him.' What's the matter with you?"

"Yeah," Sid murmured in a sullen voice.

"Quiet, Steve," I said.

Fred ran his hands through his wispy hair. "I don't know. I want to find Liz and the three presidents and get out of here, and I'm not good with stress or…people."

Sid spoke up. "It doesn't matter anyway. You got that gun from one of the underground guards—I saw on one of my cameras that you did, so don't deny it—so all you have are rubber bullets."

"Seriously?" Fred asked.

"Yep," Sid seemed cocky after that revelation.

I looked at the gun as if seeing it for the first time. "Is that right? Huh. I wonder how it would feel to get hit in the gut by one of these rubber bullets."

Sid literally gulped. "It would hurt a lot."

"Why don't you be a good sport and help us out?" I asked. I knew I wouldn't shoot Sid, not even with a rubber bullet. If I shot him, and it didn't get him to help us, then I would have to raise the ante. I could not torture him. Even if he did not know that, I did. I was willing to knock him out though. I might have to do that, but it would be one quick smack, and that would be the end of it.

Fortunately, Sid let me off the hook. He stood up warily. "Okay, I'll guide you, but when Vicky catches us, I want you to tell her that I am doing this under protest."

I grabbed Sid by the back of his collar and hauled him past me and toward the door. "That's the spirt. Let's go. Do you know where they'll take Liz?"

"I have an idea."

As we headed for the exit, I said to Fred, "Come on, Jessie James. There'll be plenty of desperadoes for you to shoot before we rescue Liz."

"Okay, but before we go," Fred's voice trailed off. He stepped up the workstation, grabbed Fred's cup of coffee, and poured it over as much equipment as he could. "I don't want Steve's replacement to come in here and track us down."

"Oh, man," Sid said. "I'm going to get stuck fixing all that."

"Not if you're in prison," I said, as I ushered him toward the exit.

Chapter Twenty-Four

Grumbling all the way, Sid guided us through the maze. We went back to the stairwell that we used to get from the fifth level to the fourth level. We went up two floors, but then the stairs stopped. We headed down a couple of hallways. We slid down a pole to the third level—a process that Fred made many negative comments about. Sid assured us he was taking us on a route that would bypass the Templetons' goons.

Sid walked us to a door on the third level that had a keypad lock on it.

"Give me two minutes, and I can bypass the system," Fred offered.

I was about to tell him to get cracking, but Sid said he knew the combination. He punched in the number, opened the door, and stepped aside. He gestured for me to go in first, so of course I pushed him in front of me and stepped through the doorway behind him.

"You should be more trusting," Sid said.

"Your boss kidnapped my father-in-law. That sort of behavior doesn't engender trust," I pointed out.

We walked into a room with a spacious open area. There were several doors along two of the other walls.

"This is probably far enough," said Sid.

I heard a rattling sound behind me and looked to see a metal wall drop into place between us and the door we had entered through. I'd been holding my gun loosely in my right hand, barrel pointed at the floor, but now I cradled it in both hands, as I spun back around to face the center of the room. Where there had once been only empty space, three security personnel now stood. They had guns drawn and pointed our way.

I wondered if those guns had rubber bullets.

Sid had led us right into a trap. I was mad at him for betraying us, at myself for allowing it to happen, and at Fred for getting me in this mess in the first place. Our traitorous guide cast a sheepish look at Fred and me, as he went slinking off to the side. He clearly had no interest in catching a stray rubber bullet. When he briefly made eye contact with me, I said, "I'm very disappointed in you."

Chapter Twenty-Five

"Nice work, Sid," said the woman standing between two men. The trio all had their guns pointed at me. It would've been nice for Fred to be a little more popular, but since I was the only one of us who was armed, I was seen as the bigger threat.

"His name is 'Steve.'" Fred sounded indignant.

They gave Sid the briefest of confused looks, then all the attention was back on me.

The woman gave off the impression that she was in charge—maybe it was because she spoke first or because she was standing in between the other two men.

She wore a dark suit, and her long hair was pulled back in a ponytail. She had the aura of a woman who had been in the Service for a while, or maybe she had been a cop. Whichever it was, she had an air of confidence. But maybe that was partially due to the two brutes who flanked her.

"Here we are," she said to me as she held her handgun at eye-level and stared down the barrel at me.

"Here we are," I repeated.

"Are you the half-blind Navy man who's been running around and beating up my guys?" her mouth held the hint of a smirk.

"It's hard to say," I replied. "I beat up a lot of guys. Can you describe yours? Were they kinda dumb and oafish looking?"

"Now see, that's the kind of mouthiness that's liable to get a man shot."

"Hey, this doesn't have to get any further out of hand," I said. "We could start dialing things way down."

"And how might we do that, Galloway?"

"My friends call me 'Adam.'"

"Okay, Adam." She gave me a nod of the head, as if greeting me for the first time. "I'm the captain of security for the Templetons—upstairs and downstairs. Name's Matilda Dupree."

"Matilda? Are you serious?" asked my father-in-law.

"Easy, Fred. We're trying to make friends here," I said. I didn't care about being friends with Matilda, but I did want to keep her talking as my mind raced for a way out of my current mess.

"I'm just saying—'Matilda' is not exactly one of your more cutting-edge names in 2026. Is she Australian?"

"What?" That made no sense to me. I didn't care, but for the record, it didn't make sense.

"Huh?" He replied.

"Would you two knock it off?" Matilda made that sound like more of a command than a question.

"He's married, just so you know. To my daughter," Fred told her.

"Okay, eww. I don't care," she said.

"Hey!" I was married, and totally off limits, but she didn't have to be rude about it.

The two henchmen stole a quick glance at each other. I guess they were trying to figure out what to make of this.

Matilda Dupree did not leave them hanging for long. "Here's the best-case scenario, Adam: You slowly put your gun on the floor and get on your knees. My guy Hank here zip ties your thumbs together behind your back, and he and Mike escort you back to your cell where your combination lock has been reprogrammed. Meanwhile, Sid and I will escort Perkins to Lab Three for a touching reunion with his granddaughter and the perpetually cranky President Nixon."

"That's a nice turn of phrase: 'perpetually cranky.' Yeah, I'd say that describes him pretty well," I said.

"Thanks," Matilda said. Her expression hardened a little, and she gestured downward with her gun, indicating her desire for me to follow her instructions.

"I've got to ask, though, is there maybe a second best scenario you could throw out here? Maybe something Fred and I could deliberate over?"

I was desperate to buy even a few extra seconds to try and think of a way out of this. Assuming they only had rubber bullets, one decently placed shot could knock me down, and it was still three against me. Even if I hadn't left my fighting stick in Sid's security office, I still would have been way outmatched.

Matilda shook her head. "No second choices; no second chances. Get on your knees, or we knock you on your back. We're going to execute my plan," she said. "The only question is how much pain you have to suffer along the way."

I didn't know what to do. I couldn't just let them lock me up; I had to rescue Liz. But I couldn't out gun three people. Suddenly, a plan popped into my head!

"There's no need to get rough," I said, as I slipped my left foot back three inches.

Matilda's eyes flickered to Fred and back, and a knowing grin played at the corner of her mouth. "Don't do it, Adam. You're not fast enough, but I will say I admire your style. Boys?" she said, addressing her two-man team, "Our Commander Galloway here was about to use his own father-in-law as a human shield."

Whereas before, Matilda motioned her gun downward to try and get me to drop my weapon, she now flicked her weapon to the side and back. "Move away from him, 'Grandpa,' before he gets you shot."

Fred complied, but he did not go quietly. "You were really going to use me as a human shield?"

"They're only using rubber bullets," I pointed out. "I mean, no, I wasn't. Of course not. What kind of guy do you take me for?"

"You two can fight later. For now: Put your gun down, Adam. Immediately."

There was nothing for me to do. There was no more wiggle room, no way to stall any longer, but I couldn't give up trying to save my daughter. Could I just go back to the cell, then crack the key code like Fred did?

I wasn't optimistic.

My stomach tightened. I was about to begin to lower myself to the floor, then start shooting. Suddenly, though, I got a reprieve, and it came from the unlikeliest source: Matilda Dupree herself.

"Ya know, I like you, Galloway. You've got moxie."

"Excuse me? 'Moxie?' Did I fall asleep and wake up in the 1940s?"

Matilda laughed politely. "You're tough, brave—I could use a guy like you on my team, and the Templetons trust me to hire who I need to get the job done. They give the orders and write the checks, but I pick my team."

"I'm…flattered, I guess."

"He's still married," Fred said to her. To me, he added, "I get so tired of your good looks."

Matilda and I both ignored him.

Dupree added, "You've got a mouth on you, Adam, but you amuse me. And when you cross the line, I'll whip you into shape. We run on discipline around here, don't we boys."

Her two thugs promptly agreed.

"You want me to…what? Betray poor Fred here?" I paused.

"Tell me you're not seriously considering this?" Fred acted appropriately outraged.

I looked from him to Matilda and back again. "A man's got to keep his options open. I mean, I do need a job."

"I can't believe this. I'm the unluckiest man alive," Fred said.

"Try being your son-in-law," I replied. To Matilda, I said, "So…what? I get to keep my gun and all of a sudden we're friends?"

"Well, there would need to be a vetting process. I'd have to insist that you lose the weapon and go back to your cell now, but I think we might be able to work something out later."

Hank—or maybe it was Mike, I didn't know one guy from the other—looked around and said to his team, "Did either of you hear that?"

I was not expecting what happened next.

Chapter Twenty-Six

Right after Matilda's lackey spoke up, the lights went out. This was followed by a lot of confused shouting on both sides. I was totally blind for a second, then I pulled off my dark glasses and stuffed them into a pocket.

Matilda shouted instructions, but she was mostly drowned out by Fred's hysterical rantings about the unfairness of the universe and the mathematical improbability that his day could get any worse.

I went low to make myself less of a target in case anyone on Matilda's team started shooting wildly. I didn't think they would, lest Fred get hit, but sometimes people make bad decisions when situations go haywire.

I threw myself in the direction of Fred's voice. As I collided with him, I heard a distinct "oof" sound that was more satisfying to me than I would ever admit to my family.

"Be quiet," I whispered to him.

Even if he had the wherewithal to remain silent— which I doubted—the emergency lighting was slowly coming up. I thought I had a temporary advantage since my eyes were a little more accustomed to dark mode, but I was quickly losing that edge.

"Why did the lights go out?" Fred asked.

"How should I know?"

There was little to no time for me to take advantage of this situation. I pointed my gun at this nearest bad guy, then I cried out in pain.

The regular lighting was suddenly back on, and that was excruciating for me. I heard a couple of grunts, as eyes had adjusted to the dark and now were a little too sensitive for the fluorescent lights. But my eyes were not a little sensitive—they were a lot sensitive. I dropped my gun as I reached for my protective eyewear.

"Galloway, just…give up before you embarrass yourself," said Matilda.

She sounded embarrassed for me, and she had reason to be. I imagine I presented a rather pathetic figure. I was on my knees, groping around with one hand for my gun. I couldn't grab my glasses with my other hand because it was shaking too badly to find the opening of my pocket. I wasn't scared, but my eyes were killing me, and my adrenaline was pumping wildly. I was rushing too much. My eyes were watering like crazy, so I couldn't see where my gun was.

"Um," Fred began, but his voice trailed off. I couldn't find fault with that. What was there to say?

Just then, I heard a door bang open. It was on the far side of the room—behind Matilda and her team.

The man who stepped into the doorway had one word for us all.

"Bully!" he shouted. And his voice was easily recognizable.

Theodore Roosevelt opened fire.

I guess he had appropriated a weapon from a guard somewhere, but wherever its origin, he was taking full advantage of it. He was firing high on purpose, and Matilda and her two men hit the deck.

Moving as quickly as I could, my fingers slipped into my pocket and tightened around my glasses. I drew them out, raked my arm across my eyes to wipe away tears of pain, and put the glasses on.

I snatched my gun off the floor and grabbed Fred by the shirt and hauled him to his feet. We began moving toward Roosevelt.

"Careful! Don't shoot Perkins!" Matilda yelled.

Stepping near one of the guards who was on one hand and two knees, I used my shin to nudge him over. I wasn't being petty; I just didn't want him to ignore his boss in the heat of the moment. It was possible that he might have decided he had a clean shot at me that would not have put Fred at risk.

Better safe than sorry.

"Well done, men!" Roosevelt bellowed as we slipped past him and moved to his left and out of the line of sight of our three enemies in the room.

Roosevelt stepped back into the hall with us, and he moved to the right.

"Nice to see you," I said, as I stuck my gun around the corner and fired blindly into the room. I figured that would discourage them from rushing to our location. Rubber bullets can inflict an extraordinary amount of pain.

"President Roosevelt! Man, you did great! That was amazing!" Fred gushed.

"Dr. Perkins, it is an honor to rescue you."

I opened my mouth to provide a little sarcasm, but I was interrupted by Matilda yelling from beyond the door. "Hey, if you guys would stop shooting at us, that would be great. Let's talk, Adam."

"I'm sorry, I'm not feeling really chatty right now. If you three will back out of that room really quickly, there's an 85 percent chance that Roosevelt and I won't shoot you."

"Don't make threats, Adam. You three are still boxed in down here like rats in a cage.

"Okay, maybe 80 percent. And stop calling us 'rats.' Roosevelt is kind of sensitive, and it's hurting his feelings."

"You're quite the pistol, Galloway," the president said. "But I think it's time for us to reunite with Mr. Lincoln. I brought one of these to facilitate our departure." He reached inside his coat pocket and pulled out a grenade.

I fired another blind shot through the doorway to discourage Matilda and her friends from getting too ambitious, and I held my free hand up to Roosevelt.

"Take it easy with that!" I said. "I don't guess they had those things back in your day, but you don't want to mess around with them. It was one of those that messed up my eyes."

"Is that so? I suppose that proves they're effective, eh?"

Roosevelt sported that big grin of his and pulled the pin.

"Nooo!" I yelled, but of course, it was too late.

Chapter Twenty-Seven

"Fire in the hole!" I yelled.

I wrapped both my arms over my glasses and squeezed my eyes shut as tightly as I could. I wanted to rescue Fred and Liz, and if I could save the three presidents, then so be it. And I would do whatever was necessary to make that happen. But if we could get away without having to kill or maim anyone, that would be the best option. Maybe I was a little too sensitive because of my own experience, but I did not want to see Matilda or her people injured by that grenade.

Matilda yelled her own instructions, then the grenade went off. As it turned out, it was a flashbang, so its destructive power wasn't nearly as great. Mostly, it created a loud noise and a blinding light—just like the flashbang that hurt me.

After it went off, I headed through the door, but Roosevelt grabbed me by the bicep.

"We need to go," he said. "We need to save Dr. Perkins." I tugged against his grasp, so he added, "We need to save Liz."

I couldn't argue that point. I spun around and the three of us ran down the hall and took the first turn that presented itself.

"There's a flap hanging down from the ceiling at the other end of the hall," Roosevelt said. "Past it, the floor slopes like a ramp. It'll take us down to the fourth level. I'm sure it will be a lot easier to get down it than it was to climb up. At the bottom there's a curve in the hall that will take us to President Lincoln."

"You've done so good, Thee," Fred said, as he huffed and puffed along. He pronounced it like the first part of Roosevelt's name, not like Fred was a visitor from the 1600s.

"What'd you call him?" I asked.

Roosevelt answered after looking at Fred and seeing him breathing so hard. "Isn't it obvious? 'Thee' is short for 'Theodore.'"

"I thought you went by 'Teddy.'"

"You were mistaken." Roosevelt sounded a little irritated.

Leave it to Fred to create a sensitive robot.

"Here we are," said Roosevelt.

Sure enough, there was a flap hanging down from the ceiling, which gave me every reason to believe that just beyond it, there was a ramp to the fourth level.

"I'll go first," said Roosevelt, as he approached the flap. "The ramp is just on the other side. Dr. Perkins, you should go next since the safest spot is in between Galloway and me. I'll be in between you and any trouble down below, and if any members of the Templetons' army come up behind us and are so frustrated that they start shooting, Galloway will be between you and the bullets."

"That's a great idea," I mumbled as Roosevelt pushed past the flap and disappeared down the ramp.

I heard him exclaim something, but his words were lost by the acoustics. I figured he probably just yelled "Tally ho" or something.

Fred went next, and I think I heard him gasp when he dropped out of sight.

I took one last look behind me, saw no signs of pursuit, and pushed the flap up out of my way.

The ramp was so close to the flap that it was virtually impossible to stop myself from sliding down it. The only challenge was to lean back so as not to fall head over heels.

When I began my slide, I saw that there was a second challenge. Roosevelt and Fred were down at the bottom, seated on the floor. Abraham Lincoln was with them, and he had his hands behind his head, elbows out. He was standing that way because there was another man with him. That man had a gun.

He looked mean.

As I slid, my gun was out, but I didn't have enough warning to aim it at the bad guy. His gun, however, swung from being pointed at Lincoln to being focused on me.

I was roughly three seconds from this guy, and each of those three seconds was hurling me right at him.

Chapter Twenty-Eight

As it turned out, I only thought I had three seconds. Even with my sore eyes, I could tell from something about the guard's body language that he planned to shoot me. No warning and no demands, he was going to shoot me because I was armed. I dropped my weapon like it was made of molten lava, and I saw his shoulders sag a little. He thought I was no longer a threat, so he relaxed.

That was when I knew I had him.

As I approached the end of the slide, I curled my legs in and flipped up to a standing position. I used my momentum from the slide to do a forward somersault. My calves landed on the guard's shoulders. I turned back and down and flipped him over me and onto his back. A quick forearm blow knocked the guy out.

I disentangled myself from the guard and retrieved my weapon, which had travelled down the slide and ended up near me, as Fred and Roosevelt stood up and joined Lincoln and me.

A huge grin spread across Lincoln's face. He grabbed Fred by the shoulders. "Dr. Perkins, it is so good to see you relatively safe and here with us! Theodore, you did a great job of securing his passage here."

"He was a champion, Abraham! You should have seen him," said Roosevelt. "He was standing up to those ruffians like a resident of Olympus. And you, sir, were superb in your timing with making the lights go off and on."

"It makes me so proud to stand here with you two and see you in action." Fred was beaming with joy.

I was incredulous. "Did anyone see what I just did?" I gestured at the unconscious guard. "The midair thing?" I pointed my index fingers at each other and made a circular motions, which prompted the three of them to look at me silently for a few seconds before going back to patting each other on the back and offering their congratulations.

"Never mind. We've got to go somewhere secure and compare notes," I said.

Roosevelt and Lincoln shared a look. "I know just the place," said Roosevelt.

I scooped up the guard's gun, stepped past Fred, who made a half-hearted attempt to reach for it, and put the weapon in Lincoln's hands.

"You don't think I could handle a gun?" asked Fred.

"I would sooner trust a one-eyed monkey."

"That's outrageous," said Roosevelt, but at least he was moving as he complained.

We headed out with Lincoln on point and me bringing up the rear. The sixteenth president took us to what would have been a dead end in any other building. In this one, there was a door that blended in almost perfectly with the wall. On the other side of that door was a breaker room. I assumed that it was from here that Lincoln cut the lights during my standoff with Matilda.

Once the four of us were inside the room, I closed the door. We were fairly cramped, but we were probably safe enough to bring each other up to speed and devise a plan.

"The last we heard, you guys were outside, leading the Templetons' security teams on a merry chase," Fred said.

Lincoln made eye contact with Roosevelt, who gestured for him to reply. "I'll start at the beginning—that always struck me as a good place to start a story. Why, that's even where the Bible starts, 'In the beginning' before getting into the substance of things," Lincoln said.

110

I bit my upper lip to keep from interrupting him. I needed him to hurry, but I thought it would just slow things down if I tried to explain that to him.

"We three presidents arrived upstairs at the Templetons' home, and Mrs. Templeton lured us inside. We were set upon by a team of ne'er-do-wells, and Liz was dropped through a trapdoor."

"I never saw how they got her out of the room," I admitted.

"Richard observed it as it happened," Roosevelt interjected. "Please, Abraham: proceed."

The sixteenth president nodded and went on. "Immediately thereafter, Galloway ran off without us and promptly got himself captured."

"That was...uncharitable," I said, but Lincoln ignored me and kept talking.

"A hidden door opened in a wall, and some men came out and grabbed Richard. They yelled at us to stay where we were. They said they would be back for both of us soon enough. I imagine they thought we were stuck since the front door was solid and locked. Once Richard was gone, though, we got a table and smashed it through a back window."

"You were very resourceful." Fred sounded like a proud dad speaking to an elementary school-aged child.

Lincoln paused for a second and beamed with joy before continuing. "We were outside for a bit, but we briefly made the acquaintance of a most accommodating fellow. He was kind enough to provide us with the gun Theodore is now using and also something called a radio. It is quite a handy piece of equipment, by the way. We used it to listen in as your whereabouts were being discussed. That's how we were able to find you."

"How were you able to navigate around in here?" I asked.

"Our helpful friend gave us an electronic map, almost like the one Galloway had on his phone. We slipped past our adversaries, broke in a window, and devised our plan to rescue you."

"You just," Fred paused and gestured in the air, "met a friendly guy and he gave you stuff?"

"Fred!" I shook my head in disbelief. "They knocked out a guard and took his gear. How is it that you can create robots with better communication skills than you have as a human being?"

"Now, Galloway, you've no cause to insult Dr. Perkins," said Lincoln. Roosevelt quickly agreed, of course.

Their gushing over Fred was exhausting.

"I can't believe you made these things that perfectly capture the personalities of our greatest presidents, and then you programmed them to hero worship you." I started to feel a little bad after I said that. I mean, it was one thing to push the guy to get with the program, but I didn't want to beat him over the head with his shortcomings.

Fred got a little squirmy and uncomfortable. "It only made sense that men of their intellect and wisdom would fully recognize my greatness."

We needed to be formulating a plan, but I couldn't let that pass. There were limits to my sympathy for Fred. "Are you kidding me?"

"You said it yourself—these android presidents are programmed perfectly. They're amazing. Besides, I also helped you solve your guilt problem over that girl when you were overseas, and I'm not even good with feelings."

"Okay, I'll give you that, but...never mind. We've got a map. I say we head to Lab Three and rescue Liz."

"Bully!" said Roosevelt. "And when we run into our enemies, we've got three guns, and I'll give them a knuckle sandwich on the side!" He shook his fist in the air.

"Knuckle sandwich. That's quite clever," said Lincoln, chuckling.

"Thank you," Roosevelt replied with a big grin.

Roosevelt's good humor left him when he noticed my expression. "What are you frowning at?" he asked.

"Nothing," I lied. I wasn't ready to talk about it yet, but something was a little off about this situation. I mean, fighting Nazis with robots as my allies was already more than a little off, but even taking that into account, there was something about this situation that was out of kilter.

I just didn't know what to do about it yet.

Chapter Twenty-Nine

Sid sat at a table with three computer monitors. He had been scrolling through security camera feeds with Vicky Templeton looming over him, literally breathing down his neck. Finally, though, he had hit paydirt. He found a camera that had Perkins, Galloway, and the two missing presidents. They were in a small room on sublevel four that controlled that floor's electrical systems.

As far as Sid was concerned, he had saved the day. He hoped Vicky saw it the same way.

"Well done, Sid!" Vicky said, as she stroked the back of his head like he was her pet dog.

There were many days when Vicky was both Sid's favorite person and his least favorite person. Somehow, she could be sweet and pretty and terrifying, all at the same time.

"I, uh, I was skeptical when you first said we needed two rooms to monitor security cameras. It just didn't make sense to me. But this backup room really came in handy after those guys nuked my system in the main room."

Sid hoped he didn't sound like a fanboy, but he wanted to be on Vicky's good side. He knew she was mad about the equipment being damaged, but it wasn't his fault that he was left alone without any protection. Besides, he'd activated his distress beacon without getting caught, and he led Perkins right to Matilda's team, so he should get Employee of the Month *if life was fair.*

But Sid knew that his life was seldom fair.

"I'm glad you found them, Sid," Vicky purred, as she continued to stroke his hair. "For your sake as well as mine. I was afraid I was going to have to murder you, and it would have been such a shame. It would be hard to replace such a good IT guy."

Sid's throat was as dry as a desert. "I just—I just want to help the team any way I can." That sounded like a lame response to a murder threat, Sid knew that, but he felt like he needed to say something.

"Can you keep tracking them?" Vicky asked, as the two men and the two androids left the room.

"Yes, ma'am."

"Good boy. That's a good boy." Vicky then stopped speaking to Sid like a dog and started addressing the departing forms on the screen in front of them. "Keep moving. Just keep moving. Time is on our side. For now."

Chapter Thirty

Probably, I should have taken the map from the robots since I was a human being with extensive military training. But they seemed to know what they were doing, and by not focusing on the map, I could continually scan our surroundings.

A few twists and turns brought us to yet another door. It opened into a small room with a pole in the middle of it. The pole extended through a circular hole in the ceiling. It was our most direct route to the third sublevel.

Fred and I eyed each other. "Time to climb," I said softly.

"Climb?" he said at normal volume. "Up there?" He pointed to the hole in the ceiling.

I raised my eyebrows, not knowing how to respond to a question with such an obvious answer. But I did have one thing to say to Fred. "If there's anyone up there, thanks for alerting them that we're here."

"Sorry."

I waved a hand at his comment. "It probably doesn't matter."

That earned me confused looks from Fred and the presidents.

"Galloway, you should go first," said Roosevelt softly.

"Right. Because I'm the most expendable in your opinion. Great robots you've got here, Fred. I see they've inherited your compassion."

"Hey, I just apologized for one thing; how much more do you want from me?"

"Nothing. Okay, Fred will follow me, then you presidents bring up the rear."

"We still haven't dealt with the problem that there is no way on God's green earth that I am going to be able to shimmy up that pole." He crossed his arms—the picture of skepticism.

I grabbed the pole and began to hoist myself up. "The key is to let your forearms do most of the work."

"Really? You think that'll work? I don't know, I have weak forearms."

"I have no idea. I was just talking to give you a false state of confidence. I don't know the physics of climbing a pole. When a pole needs climbing, I just climb it."

"Hmm," began Lincoln, "I propose that Galloway climbs to the next floor, then Theodore and I will lift Dr. Perkins off the ground. We'll get our hands under his feet, and then we will hoist him skyward toward Galloway."

"That just might work," I allowed.

"I think it will," said Fred. "Just...none of you drop me."

I climbed up to the third sublevel without incident. The presidents passed Fred up to me with a surprisingly minimal amount of complaining, followed by Lincoln, then Roosevelt.

"See?" said Fred. "There was no one up here, so it didn't matter that I talked loud."

"You didn't know that." I didn't care at this point, but I wasn't going to tell him that. As a rule, it was good to keep quiet while trying to escape from captivity. Fred needed to internalize that truth.

The room we were in offered nothing. Its sole function seemed to be to house the pole down to the next level. I walked over to the door, turned the knob as quietly as I could, and opened it.

A guard was standing right there outside the door. As he started to turn toward me, I grabbed him by the shirt and flung him toward the pole. He crashed into it and disappeared down the hole.

"You could've killed him," Fred said.

We heard a moan rise from below, so I looked at Fred and shrugged.

Roosevelt peered both ways down the hallway. "The coast is clear, gentlemen."

"We don't have far to go now," Lincoln said.

"Let's go get my granddaughter," Fred said with more enthusiasm and confidence than I had heard from him since I had awakened in his cell.

I was expecting a curveball. I decided not to be a Debbie Downer, so I didn't say anything, but there was trouble coming, and Fred was not seeing it.

Chapter Thirty-One

As we began moving through sublevel three, I motioned Roosevelt ahead of us and Lincoln behind, pantomiming that I wanted a word with Fred. They waited for him to acknowledge that he was okay with this before they moved into their positions and gave us our space.

"I'm guessing that when we get to Lab Three, there are going to be computers there, and the bad guys will have their files accessible. Can you destroy their work quickly and thoroughly?" I asked.

Liz was my number one priority, but every now and again that whole national security thing would creep back into my mind. I couldn't allow a family of money hungry Nazis to have the ability to create perfectly lifelike robots that could replace leaders and celebrities.

"Hmm, there are a lot of variables there. I'd have to access all their files and backups and wipe out everything. To guarantee that I got everything would be virtually impossible, and it will take me a while to destroy the parts that I can get to." Fred said.

I gave him a skeptical look. "Nolan has gotten me to watch enough movies and shows with a sci-fi or computer hacker angle that I know it's not impossible."

"I said 'virtually impossible,'" Fred replied.

"Right. So, when you do it, you can brag about how amazing you are."

Fred had to pause before he could think of a reply. "In fairness to me, it might be really hard."

I decided that silence was my best comeback to that comment.

We hadn't traveled very far when, lo and behold, Richard Nixon came strolling around the corner. I was apparently invisible to him, but he was thrilled to see Fred, Lincoln, and Roosevelt. In fact, Nixon was so happy to see his fellow robots and Fred that Nixon genuinely smiled. His social awkwardness was drowned out by joy. But it was a fleeting moment—he went back to looking sheepish and uncomfortable pretty quickly.

After they exchanged comments about how wonderful their blessed reunion was, Roosevelt asked, "How on earth did you escape, sir?"

"I told them I would join them," he said.

"What?" Fred's tone made his unhappiness clear.

"They were about to drill two holes in my head as part of their experiments. I said I would work with them if they wouldn't do that." Nixon beamed like he was pleased with himself.

He looked around and saw how shocked everyone was, so he leaned in and whispered, "I didn't mean it."

"And they just...let you walk around now?" asked Fred.

"They're recalibrating a machine or something, so they said I could take a walk, as long as I didn't get lost."

"They trust you? You said you were on the team, and all the sudden you can come and go as you please?" I made no effort to conceal my skepticism.

Nixon shrugged. "They've got cameras all over, and if they thought I was going to try and get away they could round me up pretty quickly."

"I messed up their surveillance system." Fred sounded proud of that.

120

"Wow, that's great!" said Nixon. "Then we can leave? I know where Liz is. I can take you right to her."

"Let's get her and go home!" said Roosevelt.

"Or we can go with Plan B," I said, as I aimed my gun at Nixon. "I can bounce a couple bullets off Nixon's face, and then we can rescue Liz."

Lincoln almost stepped between me and Nixon, but the look in my eye and the slight shake of my head gave him pause. "Now, Adam, there's no reason to start shooting the good guys. You're clearly upset, but if you shoot President Nixon, why, I'm sure that at some point the gravity of that choice will sink in, and you'll end up with the worst case of the hypo."

"What has gotten into you, Adam?" Fred added.

"Don't you guys see? We've been manipulated this whole time. Our cell was laughably easy to break out of."

"No, that was brilliant work on my part," Fred said. "I just made it look easy."

"Come on," I pushed back. "They've spent decades building an underground, five-level maze—complete with its own jail cell—they've got all these guards randomly roaming around, and they don't leave a single guy in our room to guard the crown jewel of their plan?"

"You think I'm a jewel?"

"Of their plan, yes."

"And they've got all of this surveillance down here—before you trashed it—but they never flocked to our position? Meanwhile, the two presidents were just roaming around wherever they pleased until they found us?"

"Galloway is making a strong case," Roosevelt allowed.

"And finally, we need to rescue two people before we can leave, and one of them—the programmable one—just comes waltzing down the hall without a care in the world? Color me suspicious."

Fred snapped his fingers. "They're field testing my presidents. The Templetons wanted to see them in action—interacting with people and solving problems. That's why they've given them free reign. But why'd they let us escape?"

Fred directed that question at me, but it was Lincoln who answered. "If you were a moving target, we would have to adapt more because our circumstances would keep changing. They could collect more data for their study."

"No, you folks are all mistaken. If you'll just come with me, we'll get Liz, and it will be fine," said Nixon.

"I don't trust you, Nixon. We've figured out that we've been manipulated this whole time, and this looks like a play to reel us in without Fred getting injured or the presidents getting damaged. Why don't you drop the charade?" I said.

Nixon moved his hands awkwardly in the air. "Other people may have made decisions, entirely on their own, that have reflected on me, but I won't fault them for that."

"I'm not sure what that means," Roosevelt admitted.

"It means," said Fred, "that my re-creation of Nixon is no better at accepting responsibility than the original was. But in this case I would say it wasn't his fault. Adam's right: The Templetons reprogrammed President Nixon."

"Richard, didn't you fight the Nazis in World War Two?" Fred asked. "Why would you join them now?"

Could Fred break through the reprogramming with logic and morality? Could Nixon reprogram himself? It was strange to think about.

"I was in the Pacific Theater. I fought the Japanese. But this isn't about politics. It's about taking power so we can do the right things."

"Without pesky things like democracy, freedom, and morality getting in the way," I said. "Fred, can you reprogram him?"

"Don't touch me!" Nixon roared.

"Oh, you're definitely going to be touched," I said. Then I shot Richard Nixon.

Chapter Thirty-One

I popped two slugs at his left thigh. He howled in pain, as his leg was violently forced out from under him. He toppled onto his face. He groaned and rocked back and forth—still facedown—in apparent agony, which was kind of fascinating since he was not a man but a machine. Was he truly reacting to a physical sensation of pain, or was he just acting that way because he was programmed to mimic how the real Nixon would respond if he was shot in the thigh? The bullets were rubber, but from my close proximity and the high speed at which the bullets traveled, the pain they could induce was tremendous.

"Can you fix him?" I asked Fred.

"I don't know. How much damage do those bullets do?"

"Not from the bullets," I said, exasperated at Fred for not reading my mind. I must admit I wasn't always fair with him. "Can you fix the brainwashing the Templetons gave him?"

"What's the quickest way?" Fred's voice trailed off. He was talking to himself. "Quick—grab him by the shoulders and lift him up," Fred ordered the other two presidents.

Roosevelt and Lincoln scrambled to comply. Nixon moaned, then whimpered as they hauled him to his feet.

Fred stepped behind the turncoat president and began pressing different spots on the back of his robot head.

"Leave me alone," Nixon said. His speech was slurred.

Fred didn't bother to reply—he just continued working. A section of Nixon's hair flipped up. Fred stuck two fingers inside the robot's head. The inventor pressed in and paused for a few seconds. He pulled his hand out, as Nixon's eyes rolled up and, well, if he were human, I would have said he passed out. He would have fallen to the ground if his fellow presidents had not been holding onto him.

"Give it a few seconds," Fred said.

"What did you do to him?" I asked.

Before Fred could answer, Nixon's head lifted up, and his eyes opened wider than normal, like he was terrified. He licked his lips and mumbled. "Taxes…Checkers…good dog…YOU WON'T HAVE RICHARD NIXON TO KICK AROUND ANYMORE!"

"Fred, can you do something more here, or should I call an exorcist?"

"What's going on? Where'd you guys come from? Dr. Perkins! It's good to see you! What's happening? Ah, why does my leg hurt so bad?"

"I had to give you a reset, President Nixon. You should be fine now."

"Thank you so much, sir."

"It was the least I could do," Fred said.

"Where does this leave us? What do we do now?" asked Lincoln.

"Can you get us back to Lab Three?" I directed my question to Nixon.

He scowled at me. "How in the world would I be able to do that?" He turned to the other three, as if looking for support in his belief that my question was ridiculous.

"Let's assume that's a 'no,'" I said.

"If you're looking for the route to Lab Three, I would be happy to take you. But lose the guns first, boys."

My eyes darted from the source of those words to Roosevelt and back.

"Hi, Matilda," I said.

"I hope there are no hard feelings about the grenade." Roosevelt smiled weakly.

Chapter Thirty-Two

Matilda walked down the hall toward us, and she wasn't alone. She was flanked by four guards, two on each side. I stole a glance in the other direction and saw four more bad guys approaching us. We were boxed in. Trapped. Three guns vs nine.

"Why is my leg bleeding?" Nixon sounded agitated.

"Eww," I said at the sight of a dark, non-blood type fluid running down the outside of Nixon's pants below the rubber bullet wounds I inflicted.

"What can we do about that?" I asked Fred.

He frowned at Matilda. "I guess the best we can do for now is tie it off above the wounds to slow down the loss of fluid."

My assumption was that he did not want to do anything that would help the bad guys understand the inner workings of his robots. Surely, Barry Templeton knew a lot, but Fred wasn't going to make things any easier for them. Or maybe Fred just didn't have the equipment he needed for a serious repair job.

I wasn't used to giving Fred the benefit of the doubt, but then I wasn't used to life like robots either. Anything was possible these days.

"May I," I asked Matilda, as I gestured toward Nixon's leg.

Matilda pondered it for a second or two, then responded with a curt nod. "Put the guns down first."

127

I frowned, but I complied with her orders. I gently placed my gun on the floor. Roosevelt and Lincoln did the same after an approving nod from Fred.

Reaching over with my right hand, I grabbed ahold of my left sleeve up near the shoulder and gave a quick, hard yank. I tore some cloth off and kneeled next to Nixon, so I could wrap it around his leg above where the damage was done. I didn't know how much this would staunch the flow of liquid, but it was the best that I could do.

"Does that help?" I asked.

"My leg really hurts," Nixon replied.

"I'm sorry I shot you."

"What?" Nixon was appropriately outraged.

"Hey, I only shot you twice. It's not like I emptied the clip."

"You shot me twice?!" Nixon repeated. "Why did you shoot me at all?"

"It…seemed like a good idea at the time."

Nixon turned to Lincoln. "Why did he shoot me?"

Lincoln shook his head and whispered, "Not now."

"That was pretty impressive—ripping that sleeve off. It's like something you see in movies but not in real life. It's a tough thing to do," Matilda said.

"I have my shirts tailored with loose threads for occasions such as this."

Matilda shook her head. "Enough of this nonsense. You two have been wanting to see what's inside of Lab Three for long enough. We're going to escort you right through the front door."

She gestured with her gun for all of us to go past her and head down the hall.

As the three presidents started walking, Nixon said, "My leg hurts."

"It'll hurt worse if I have to shoot it some more. Keep moving," Matilda said.

"Now, ma'am, there is no need to be so adversarial. We're all happy to go see Lab Three and check on Miss Liz. She's there, right?" Lincoln asked.

"Yes. You'll all be together, and the Templetons can decide what to do with you."

Fred and I fell into step behind the presidents. As I crossed next to Matilda, I winked at her.

"I saw that!" said Fred.

And that was when I risked everything.

Chapter Thirty-Three

I was never going to get within a closer proximity to Matilda. If I didn't make a grab for her gun now, the opportunity would be lost. The wink was simply an attempt to make her brain process something besides the physical threat I posed. Fred's outrage was icing on the cake. Her gaze flickered toward him for just a split second, but conveniently, it was the split second when I started making my move.

Was it luck or divine intervention? I guess I'll leave that question for the philosophers. I will note that I had been praying silently almost nonstop since Liz was taken, which I guess makes it clear that I hadn't prayed that much before then—when only Fred was kidnapped.

I am not a perfect man.

Anyway, the timing was perfect, so I grabbed Matilda by the wrist, twisted it, and slid her gun from her grasp. I pulled her forward and slipped behind her. With one arm around her neck, I rested the gun against the base of her skull.

"Listen up, guys: Drop your guns now, or there's going to be a job opening for your chief of Nazi security."

The guards looked at each other, unsure of what to do. I couldn't outshoot all eight of them. If just one of them opened fire, I would probably twitch and shoot Matilda, which I had no desire to do, but more importantly, it would stop me from saving Liz.

"Protect Fred!" I snapped at the presidents. I was worried that one of the guards would violate their standing orders and try to put Fred in the position I had Matilda in.

The three presidents jumped into protective positions around their beloved creator and ushered him past the guards, removing him from any potential line of fire.

"Matilda, I would appreciate it if you would save your life by having your boys put their guns on the floor."

"How about I just shoot him?" said one of the guards. He was a tall guy with spiky hair and a surprisingly ugly face.

"How about you follow orders," replied Matilda.

"Yeah, Spike, follow orders," I said, then I decided I made a mistake based on the guy's reaction to me. I should have left my mouth shut, but that was a thing I sometimes struggled with.

The man's eyes blazed anger at me. His breathing got louder and deeper. It was crystal clear that he really wanted to shoot me. Fortunately, Matilda was an authority he seemed to respect. He contented himself by cursing at me, then he put his gun on the floor.

"You guys back up," I said with a gentler tone. Spike's reaction had spooked me a bit. I was really close to seeing Liz, and I did not want to screw it up by pushing one of these guys into an unpredictable action that would lead to chaos.

Fortunately, they backed away without incident. The three presidents gathered up their weapons.

"Each of you take one gun, even you Fred. And then, Fred, dismantle the rest of the weapons."

"What makes you think I can do that?"

"They're mechanical objects, and you're a mechanical genius."

"Really?"

"Don't tell me you're doubting yourself," I said.

"Well, of course not. I'm just surprised that you're admitting it."

"We're about to see Liz, and I'm feeling magnanimous."

Fred sprang into action, and I was impressed with how quickly he figured out how to dismantle the guns.

When he had finished his work, I thought about complimenting him, but instead I simply said, "Let's go."

I held onto Matilda, as we backed down the hallway, keeping an eye on the unhappy guards as we went. Roosevelt and Lincoln were in the lead with Fred and Nixon in the middle.

"I'll take you to Lab Three, but you might not like what you find there," said Matilda.

Chapter Thirty-Four

"If Perkins would just cooperate, all our troubles would just go away. Poof! Like a vapor of smoke," Matilda grumbled her words as we walked down the hall.

"I'm guessing that you read a file, or got a briefing, or heard Barry Templeton talk about Fred, right?" I asked.

"Yeah."

"Then you should realize that cooperating is not his strength. Being insufferable? Yeah, that's more of his go-to personality trait."

"Very funny," Fred said.

"Your attitude toward Dr. Perkins is most uncharitable," said Lincoln.

"I agree. If nothing else, you should try to show some class, Galloway," Roosevelt added.

"You're a jerk," Nixon said.

I should have shot you more was the phrase that popped into my head. Out loud, all I said was, "Which way, Matilda?"

"Left."

We took the hall to our left, and roughly one hundred feet later, Matilda stopped abruptly. It was an irritating move because I was still walking backwards with her. I kept one arm around her neck and a gun pointed at the back of her head, as I continued to scan the hallway behind us. When she stopped, my momentum caused me to slightly choke her. She grunted but did not complain.

I instinctively felt a pang of remorse at making her uncomfortable, and that was what was irritating. I felt bad because I'm not an abusive person, but she had brought that pain on herself by stopping without warning. I didn't want to feel sorry for her. She was my prisoner—she was the key to finding and rescuing Liz.

"We're here," Matilda said. "Lab Three."

"We need to devise a plan," said Roosevelt, who, like his fellow presidents, had a gun at the ready.

"I have a plan," I said.

I maneuvered halfway around Matilda without loosening my grip and kicked open the door to the lab.

I pushed Matilda through the doorway and used her as a human shield as I surveyed the scene. The room had multiple computer workstations. There were also three contraptions that leaned upright but looked like they could be tilted back to serve as diagnostic beds. I assumed that they were there in case the bad guys wanted to study all three presidents at once. There were tables and chairs and machines of various shapes and sizes. Were they for running tests of some sort? I didn't know. Barry and Vicky Templeton were in the room and looking appropriately menacing, and there were six security guards with them— four were wearing their twenty-first century Nazi uniforms, and the other two were in suits and ties.

Best of all, across the room and sitting in a chair sat Liz!

She jumped up when she saw us, causing the guard standing next to her to give her an angry glare.

"Dad! Grandpa!" She beamed with joy.

"Isn't this a touching reunion? How sweet," said Vicky.

"I hate to rain on the dawn of the Fourth Reich. Okay, that's not true. I'm delighted to foil your Nazi plans. Fred's not going to join you, and we fixed Nixon. Now, we can do the rest of this the easy way or the hard way. I'm taking my daughter, and we're all leaving."

I'm not sure what I was expecting in response to that monologue, but whatever it was, I got something I didn't anticipate.

"Well done, Galloway. You passed every test. You're hired," said Barry. He acted quite comfortable with the situation, which bothered me. It meant he believed he had the upper hand.

"What test?"

"We aren't just trying recruit Mr. Perkins. We want you too. We try to be discreet about who knows what with our operation, and once you found out about the presidents, we saw an opportunity. Your military and martial arts training make you very well qualified to help with our security. Um, are your eyes going to get better?"

"Yeah, my eyes are already better. I just wear the glasses because they're cool. But it doesn't matter because I don't want to be a Nazi flunky."

"Oh, don't worry, Handsome. We have bigger plans for you."

"Calm down, Vicky," said Barry, sounding irritated. To me, he said, "We want you to take over all security for this whole facility—the house and all the sublevels. You would also be in charge of the planning and conduct of all our clandestine operations."

Barry's gun had been pointing at me since I walked in the room, but I wasn't worried because I still had my human shield.

"What about Matilda?" I asked.

"What about her?" Barry replied, as if she meant nothing to him at all.

Then he fired his weapon.

Chapter Thirty-Five

Barry Templeton fired two slugs that slammed against Matilda's chest and shoulder areas. She grunted with the impact of the first shot, and the noise she made morphed into a groan when the second of the rubber bullets hit her. She was flung back against me, and she would have slid to the floor if not for me holding her up.

"What is wrong with you?" yelled Fred. "Are you crazy?"

"She's not dead, but now you know we're not playing around," Barry replied.

"I figured you weren't playing around when you kidnapped me." Fred shook his head in disgust. "Having to deal with…people…is just the worst."

"You might want to modify your tone, Mr. Perkins," said Vicky. "My husband had to watch his temper when he worked for you, but it's there, so you might not want to push him."

Barry swung his gun over and aimed it at Fred. The malicious grin the bad guy suddenly sported was not an attractive look.

"You can't shoot me. I thought this was all about me," Fred protested.

"You think everything is about you," Vicky said.

I nodded in agreement but said nothing.

Barry, however, was not reluctant to speak. "You can't have it both ways, *Boss*." Barry's voice dripped with sarcasm over that last word. "Either you're going to work with us, or you're not. We offered you money, we locked you up, we kidnapped your granddaughter, and you still refuse to cooperate. Maybe we should just shoot you here and now, and I'll just figure out the tech myself."

"Easy, Honey," said Vicky.

"I'm tired of taking it easy, and I'm tired of Fred's ego. I can figure out the androids. I'm smart too, you know."

"Oh, come on. You would need IQ steroids to even get up to mediocre," Fred said.

Fred was proving to be a great distraction, but his abysmal people skills were about to get him shot. Barry was so mad that his gun hand was shaking. Clearly, rage was surging through the guy's body. Well, it was clear to the rest of us, but Fred gave no indication that he had any idea of the fire he was playing with.

"Liz," I spoke in a casual, conversational tone of voice. Liz was across the room from me, so speaking loudly enough for her to hear meant I needed to speak loud enough for everyone to hear, but I was hoping Barry was too focused on Fred to realize what I was up to. "You don't need to say the words, but I want you to think through what Logan tells you every time he shows us a magic trick."

My son loved card tricks. And he was quite good at them because he had genuine ability at sleight of hand. Almost every time, his shtick included three words of instruction for Liz.

Her eyes widened, as it dawned on her what I wanted her to do.

"What are you talking about?" asked Vicky.

"Can we focus on you telling Barry not to shoot me?"

Bless you, Fred, for your self-absorbed ego.

"Now!" I yelled to Liz.

She did exactly what I wanted her to. Nolan's typical pattern for a card trick included holding the stack in front of him and saying to Liz, "Hit the deck."

Obviously, the meaning was different here, but she got the message. She slammed into the guard standing next to her, then dove down and away from him.

I took the gun I had pointed at Matilda's head and fired too quickly at Barry. I wanted to hit him in the chest, but instead I only got his shoulder. It was enough to spin him around and send him to the floor.

I slid behind a table and pushed it over in front of me, using it as a shield. Everybody else moved for cover at that point with presidents and bad guys sending rubber bullets in every direction.

"I want you all to know," began Roosevelt, "regardless of how this shall turn out, it has been a supreme blessing to serve alongside each of you. Even you, Galloway."

"I concur," said Lincoln. "You men have comported yourselves with valor and dignity throughout these proceedings. It has been my honor to stand with you—and now kneel behind this chair as I endeavor to not be shot. It's an inconvenient time to be a tall man, I'll tell you plainly."

As if on cue, a bullet knocked the stovepipe hat off his head.

Nixon cleared his throat and said, "It's 'Dr.' Perkins."

"What?" I couldn't help but ask.

Bullets were coming at me from two different directions.

"The woman called him 'Perkins,' but it's 'Doctor Perkins.' People should get it right and be respectful."

"You're quite right, Richard," said Lincoln.

"I don't want this to be the last conversation I'm involved in before I die," I said.

At that moment, I did not have a direct shot at anyone. I fired a couple of rounds at one of the machines, intending to destroy it. My plan worked. Sparks flew out of the device, then there was a popping sound and part of the front of it exploded.

I was glad to create a new problem for the Templetons, but I knew I couldn't shoot up all the equipment. I only had a limited number of bullets.

Liz was hiding behind some machinery, safe for the moment, but we were definitely in a predicament. Two of the guards were down that I knew of. Barry had moaned a couple of times, and he seemed to be neutralized as a threat. But that still left Vicky, up to four guards, and maybe Matilda. Plus, there were still eight thugs in the hall. One of the presidents had shut the door, so the eight might not be an immediate threat, but I had no idea how to get Liz, Fred, and the robots to safety.

Chapter Thirty-Six

Fred was keeping his head down behind a couple of chairs. He was halfway under a desk with a computer on it. I caught his eye. I pointed at the computer, held up a fist, and turned it over. He looked confused, so I repeated the gesture.

"What? You want me to get on the computer and ruin their research?"

I rubbed my free hand over my face in disgust. "Yes. But I didn't want you to advertise it."

"Oh, right," he said. He reached blindly up to the desktop and pulled the keyboard down.

"Matilda! Stop him! Stop Perkins!" yelled Vicky.

Lincoln fired a shot at Vicky, but he had a bad angle and missed. It was a wonder that none of us had been hit yet. Everybody on both sides was playing defense instead of offense. People were keeping themselves safe behind furniture and equipment, rather than exposing themselves for the sake of a good shot.

Matilda had been laying on her side, but at the sound of her name, she stirred a bit.

"Did you hear me? I said stop him!" ordered Vicky.

Matilda had a great angle on Fred. She could have shot him if she had a gun, but she didn't, which Vicky seemed to not remember. Or maybe Vicky wanted Matilda to attack Fred with her bare hands. Of course, Fred had picked up a gun when we disarmed the guards in the hallway, so he could shoot Matilda if she became a threat. That is to say, he could do that if he had the first clue about using a gun.

Matilda pulled herself up to her hands and knees. "Your husband shot me, and you think I'm going to follow your orders?"

Vicky's reply was dismissive. "He had to get you out of the way, and they were rubber bullets."

"The pain…is excruciating."

"Well, there'll be more where that came from if you don't get up and do your job."

"Men," Matilda said, "Stand down."

Chapter Thirty-Seven

"Ya know," I shouted out to anyone who would listen, "life sure is funny sometimes. I mean, I spent all those years in the Navy, sometimes on missions I still can't talk about, and I gave that up for a simpler lifestyle. Thought I'd be a singer, but that didn't work out. Figured I'd put in a little time with the fam. And here I am, hanging out with my daughter and my father-in-law, but this just isn't what I had in mind."

"Will you shut up?" asked an overly irritated guard.

A couple of slugs impacted the other side of the table I was hiding behind.

"I just thought it might be helpful if we took a few minutes and calmed down. Maybe got to know each other a little as people." In retrospect, I see that I talk when I shouldn't.

"I said 'stand down,'" repeated Matilda. "We're not going to get what we want from Perkins, so the Templetons aren't going to be able to pay us in full. And if Barry's going to shoot me for being in the way, then we can't trust them. This has gone on long enough. Everybody put your guns down."

I heard the blissful sound of guns gently landing on the floor. I saw Fred peek around from his position of cover, nod his head, then slide up into a seat with his keyboard in hand. He would be a lot more effective at destroying their intel if he could actually see the computer screen.

Just then a single shot rang out. I heard Lincoln howl in pain and grab his left hand.

Fred ducked for cover, which interrupted his work thwarting the plans of our supervillains.

"Hanson, stop!" Matilda yelled.

"At least one of you is loyal," sneered Vicky.

"It's over; let it go," Matilda said to Hanson. "We're not going to get paid."

"It's not about the money for me."

"So, you're really a Nazi?" Nixon sounded incredulous.

I checked my clip to see how many shots I had left. I was disappointed with what I found. "You've got to be kidding me," I mumbled.

"It's about…Vicky," said the guard named Hanson.

"Ah, right. He literally is a Nazi lover," I said.

"The real Nazis were horrible. I should know; I lived through them. You wannabes are just embarrassingly stupid," said Nixon.

I peeked over the table I was hiding behind and saw Hanson, gun at the ready, walking over to where Vicky was standing.

"Look," said Matilda, "Everyone else is done with this. The rest of the team is done, Barry crawled out of here during the confusion, it's over."

Vicky and Hanson quickly scanned the room, but Matilda was right. Barry had slipped away during all the shooting.

"That…coward." Vicky wore a furious expression.

"He doesn't deserve you. He never did," said Hanson.

He turned toward Vicky so he could console her.

I knew I needed to take advantage of the moment. I stuck my gun in the back of my waistband and hurled myself at Hanson. I swung my leg up and wrapped it around his left side. I pulled one of his arms in front of him, and curled under it, hooking my heel around the left side of his head, I let my body weight bring him forward to the floor. Once we were grounded, I twisted his arm until he cried out and dropped his gun. Then, I twisted some more because I was having a bad day, and he was a bad person.

I knocked him out and reached for his gun, but Vicky kicked it away. She watched it slide across the floor, which was a mistake because that gave me the time to retrieve my weapon from behind my back.

"Drop it, Vicky," I said.

"We'll just shoot each other, and you won't win."

"I'll shoot you, and you'll drop your weapon, or you'll shoot me, and my three favorite presidents will bounce bullets off you from all kinds of directions."

"Roosevelt is tending to Lincoln, and Nixon is out of bullets. It's a standoff."

I nodded. "You're absolutely right. Oh, except that I received advanced training in the Navy in enduring pain. Also, I've experienced torture. I'm convinced I can withstand getting shot by you long enough to hit you in the chest, stomach, and at least one kneecap before I go down. You squeeze that trigger, and you aren't walking out of here. You'll be carried out to an ambulance."

With a noise of frustrated disgust, Vicky lowered her weapon. Matilda, visibly in pain, had been quietly shuffling up behind her and now took the gun. Vicky gave Matilda a sullen look but said nothing.

Matilda said, "You could've shot her three times before going down. Yeah, right." She punctuated her remark with an unattractive snort.

I ignored her. "I'm glad you did that," I said to Vicky. "I've been out of bullets for a little while now."

"I hate you so much."

Chapter Thirty-Eight

"Eureka! I did it!" Fred crowed in triumph. "Everything the Templetons have on android technology has either been erased, or it's about to be. I infected everything in their network and in the cloud."

Fred held the keyboard over his head like it was a trophy. His face beamed with joy. I hadn't seen him this happy since a scientist he knew from grad school got outed for plagiarism and lost a cushy research job. When Fred was in a good mood, it wasn't always a pretty thing. But today was a good day for us, and—dare I say it—a good day for America.

"There's no way you could have attacked all our files that quickly. This isn't some stupid movie," sneered Vicky.

Fred had put the keyboard down and raised an index finger in disagreement. "I think what you meant to say was that a lesser genius could not have done it so fast. But while it is surprising that Barry didn't make it more clear to you, I'm pretty much in a league of my own."

"In fairness to Dr. Perkins, he is an extraordinary genius," said Roosevelt. "It's a true pleasure to know him."

"There's nothing quite like having three robot presidents with a serious case of hero worship wired into them." I was almost past being amazed by Fred's ego.

"Androids," said the three presidents simultaneously.

"What do we do about flash drives, paper and ink notes, and whatnot?" I directed my question at Fred.

"Do I have to figure out everything?"

Just then, the door to the hallway flew open, and bad guys began pouring in. I swung my empty gun at them, but it was Matilda who saved the day. "Stand down, boys. The party's over."

Vicky shrugged herself out of Matilda's grasp, which wasn't hard to do since Matilda was still clearly struggling from the pain of being shot with rubber bullets.

"It's not over!" yelled Vicky, seething with anger. "Shoot them all, especially Matilda the traitor."

"That's why this is over." Matilda responded to Vicky's anger with remarkable calm. "The Templetons can't be trusted. Barry shot me just for being in his way, then he ran away like the little coward that he is. And he was the only one we could relate to. He was just in this for the money. Everybody needs a paycheck. But the paycheck isn't coming, fellas. Perkins won't cooperate. There's no money to be made here. There's nothing left, except Vicky being a Nazi. We aren't Nazis, and we aren't getting paid. Let's get out of here."

"It's not over for me!" Hanson cried. He had awakened, and now he was getting up from the floor. "I'm still with you, Vicky. And the Nazis--"

He stopped talking abruptly and slumped back to the floor, as I wacked him on the head with the butt of my gun.

The rest of the guards slowly began to drift out of Lab Three. When it was clear that things were safe, Liz ran out from her hiding place. I engulfed her in a hug. Next, she ran to her grandfather and hugged him too.

After slowly pulling away from him, she approached the three presidents. Lincoln smiled shyly, put his arm across his waist and gave a low, formal bow. "Miss Liz, I am delighted that you are okay," he said and smiled broadly.

Roosevelt beamed at her, then smothered her in a big bear hug, laughing the whole time.

Finally, she turned to Nixon, and he gazed at her sheepishly before sticking his hand out and giving her what had to have been the most awkward and stiff handshake of her life.

When she was done with them, she came back over to me, and I put my arm around her shoulders. She seemed taller than she had been this morning.

For a second, I felt old, but I shook it off to focus on the business at hand.

"Now, about those hard copies and backup files," I said.

"Hmm, said Lincoln, "I think a nice big fire could potentially solve a lot of problems."

"You would burn my house down?"

I answered for Lincoln, "On the one hand, I don't have a lot of sympathy for a Nazi kidnapper, but on the other hand—oh, who am I kidding? I only have the one hand for this. Come on, Vicky, you're not going to be using this house anyway—you're going to grow old in prison."

"Not if we burn away all the evidence," Roosevelt pointed out.

"Excellent point, Commissioner Roosevelt," said Nixon. He sounded kind of smug about it, as if Nixon had argued against torching the house and Roosevelt was backing him up. But of course, that hadn't happened. Nixon was a peculiar bird.

"I would say we are faced with a dilemma. We have to turn Mrs. Templeton over to the authorities, and we have to keep ourselves and our origins out of the limelight. I am open to suggestions," said Roosevelt.

"Matilda could go and give a full report to the police," suggested Nixon.

"Again, though, we are faced with the dilemma of the evidence. It is best to destroy all the records, but then there is no proof of a motive," said Roosevelt.

"And before you get ahead of yourselves, no, I'm not reporting anything," said Matilda. "Great plan: Let me explain to the cops that I was involved in a kidnapping." She acted pretty disgusted with the idea, and I couldn't blame her.

"Hey! You all need to wait a minute!" yelled Fred. Immediately, the three presidents acted like they were on high alert. If something bothered Fred, it bothered them. He was yelling at the guards who were slipping out of the room in ones and twos.

"Let them go and count your blessings," I said. I was delighted that they were loyal enough to Matilda that they gave up when she told them to, and I didn't want to provoke them when they still outnumbered and outgunned us.

Fred visibly relaxed, so the presidents did too, and the guards sped up their exodus. Soon, it was just Liz, me, Fred, the three presidents, Matilda, Vicky, and the unconscious Hanson.

"Here's some advice: don't see what's not here," said Matilda. "I didn't become a hero. I just don't like getting double crossed, and I don't like betting on a losing horse. I have zero interest in turning myself in. I was part of kidnapping Perkins, and I was part of saving your necks, so I figure we're even. I'm walking out of here. What you do with Vicky is your problem."

I nudged the lump on the floor that was Hanson and asked, "What about him?"

"He's Vicky's problem." And with that, Matilda headed for the door.

She stopped right as she was about to exit and turned back around to look at me. "If you decide to torch the place, wait for fifteen minutes. I'm going to message whoever is left among my people to tell them to get out, and I want to clean out my locker."

I nodded, then said, "Hey, Matilda," She was already moving on, but she held up at the sound of her name. "If in the future you ever happen to see one of my kids anywhere, go the other way. Immediately."

"I can live with that," she said.

"Yes. Yes, you can."

She smirked as she instantly recognized my implied threat, and then she was gone.

We were quiet for a few seconds before Vicky broke the silence. "What do you plan to do with me? You can't take me to the cops without giving away your secrets, and Roosevelt and Lincoln won't let you kill me."

Fred started talking, and it was not until then that I realized that he had been hunched over the computer, typing away on the keyboard. "I'll tell you this," he said to Vicky, "Whatever you end up doing, you won't have much money to do it with. I hacked into your accounts, and I am making donations left and right with your money."

"What! You can't do that!" She lunged in Fred's direction, but Roosevelt and Lincoln grabbed her well before she could reach him.

"You shouldn't have kidnapped me, and you shouldn't have held my granddaughter against her wishes. Maybe the cops arrest you, and maybe they don't, but you won't have the resources to be a threat to me or my family again."

"You couldn't have hacked into our accounts that quickly. It's impossible."

"If I didn't have to stop and remind you people every ten minutes that I am uniquely brilliant, then I'd probably be back home by now."

"I'm going to make you all pay for this!" she shouted, as she squirmed against the grasp of two of the presidents.

"No, you won't," said Roosevelt, using a tone that the real Roosevelt had probably used on his children. "Because if I ever see you or that scoundrel of a husband of yours, I will take you into my personal custody, shave my moustache, escort you to the local constabulary, and level all manner of charges against you. I'll put you and your husband under such a microscope that the authorities will be able to count the dandruff flakes on your husband's head."

That shut her up.

Liz leaned into me and whispered, "Why would he shave his moustache?

I whispered back, "Probably so he wouldn't look like Theodore Roosevelt. Instead, he would just look like a dude with thick glasses and a bad haircut."

Nixon snorted, then he coughed to try and cover it up.

"Ma'am?" Lincoln addressed Vicky, "I would advise you to go find your husband and tell him to give us a wide berth. There are other presidents where we come from, and I can think of more than one who would be more than happy to put a bullet in you both for what you've done to Dr. Perkins and sweet Liz."

As she processed the threat made by America's sixteenth president, Hanson moaned and lifted his head. "What's going on?"

I grabbed him by the front of his shirt and jerked him to his feet. "You and Vicky are going to run away together."

"Cool," he mumbled distractedly, as he shook himself free of my grasp.

"Yeah," I continued, "you're going to run away, straight to Barry."

"Oh," his disappointment was apparent.

I watched them both leave and wondered if letting two Templetons and one unrepentant lackey escape was the best plan we could have made. Again, I found myself silently praying that God would protect me from the consequences of a potentially stupid choice.

"News flash," announced Fred, still sitting at the computer, "The walls, floors, and ceilings are all fire resistant."

"Hmm, that does complicate matters," said Roosevelt.

"No, it does the exact opposite. It means we can torch a bunch of rooms, and destroy any records hidden in them, with little danger of the fire spreading outside this house," I pointed out.

"But if we destroy the house, won't the Templetons get a ton of money from their insurance?" asked Liz.

"Where'd you learn about homeowner's insurance?" I was impressed. I wanted to think of her as my little girl, but she was becoming less so every day.

"Mom talked about it with me and Nolan."

"I would imagine the Templetons won't want to answer any questions about the layout of the house or the circumstances of the thorough arson job we're going to do," said Fred. "I think they're going to run far away."

Chapter Thirty-Nine

A few days later, we were sitting as a family in the living room. It was Friday night. Elaine had returned from her business trip, and Nolan was spending the weekend at home before heading back to college. The two of them were listening as Liz, Fred, and I told them about our crazy adventure.

Fred and I had discussed the pros and cons of keeping the story to ourselves, but I was against that plan. While I was in the Service, there were things I couldn't tell Elaine for security reasons. I promised her when I left the Navy that I would never keep secrets from her again. Plus, I didn't want Liz to feel the pressure of keeping the truth of such a big and potentially traumatic experience from her mother or Nolan.

And if the Templetons ever came sniffing around, which I highly doubted, I wanted everyone in my family to have their guard up.

Fred and Liz added a few details here and there, as I told my story. When I had wrapped it up, Elaine and Nolan sat quietly, processing it all.

It was Elaine who spoke up first. "I asked a simple question about why my husband and father were all of a sudden getting along, and your explanation was…all that?"

"Remarkable, huh?" I replied.

"I'm not sure I'm ready to accept one hundred percent of what you told us."

"Which parts do you have a problem with?" asked Fred.

"It might be easier to list which parts I believe."

"Okay." I gestured for her to share.

"I...believe we have a daughter named 'Liz.'"

"I believe that Mr. Templeton had a problem working for Grandpa," Logan chimed in.

"My boy!" I said. "Such keen insight!"

"Hey!" Fred protested.

"Come on, y'all," Elaine said. "Talking robots? Kidnapping?"

"First of all, they're androids," Fred pointed out.

"Whatever," she replied.

"Thank God you're home," I said to my wife.

"I have a question," Liz said. "I already asked Dad this, but really it's more of a Grandpa question. Why'd you make a Nixon android? I mean, his personality. Wow." She shook her head.

Fred shrugged. "In case of an emergency, I wanted a president who could drive in modern traffic."

Liz looked as confused as I felt. There were other presidents who could drive who would have been much easier to get along with. Liz opened her mouth but was interrupted by a knock on the door.

"That must be the pizza. Nolan, please grab it, would you?" asked Elaine.

Nolan jumped out of his seat and ran to the door, not bothered in the least that there was a large chair in his way. Elaine started to protest, but it was too late to stop him from executing a no-hands cartwheel over the chair. He landed safely on his feet and kept moving toward his target without a word.

Elaine's eyes blazed at me. "I told you there would come a day when he would start doing what you do. I am not pleased."

"He's mastered a difficult and useful skill," I said proudly.

"How about 'dangerous and pointless?' I think that's what you meant. I want you to talk to him."

"Yes, ma'am."

Liz was grinning at me, so I glared at her in fake anger.

Nolan opened the door and stepped back, speechless.

"Is something wrong, Honey?"

"Mom, it's, um, the pizza, but it's not the pizza guy."

Elaine looked at me with alarm. She pointed at me and flicked her finger toward the door, but I was already moving. By the time I got next to Nolan, I had removed my gun from an ankle holster and had it in hand.

I looked through the doorway and smiled.

"Elaine, there's someone I would like you to meet."

I turned toward the three of them. Liz was grinning and scurried our way. Fred was smiling too, but he remained seated as he typed on his phone. Elaine came over warily and joined us at the door.

There was a man on our doorstep holding two boxes of pizza. He said, "I saw a gentlelady leave these boxes at your door, and I decided they smelled too wonderful to leave on the ground. I now present them to you, the Lady of the House."

The man balanced both boxes with one of his big hands. With the other hand, he took his hat off and swept it in front of him as he offered a deep bow.

I said, "Elaine, Nolan, Liz, meet the Father of our Country. General Washington, would you care to join us for dinner?"

Acknowledgements

I would like to thank my lovely wife, Jill, for her support for all my writing endeavors. Her love, encouragement, and kind words always mean a lot. Being able to share my victories with her, such as a book I just finished writing, is a blessing that I do not take for granted. It is also great that I get to benefit from her intelligence and creative talents, including her work on the cover art for this book and several others.

Word Weavers International is an organization of Christian writers that provides constructive feedback for members. I am part of an online chapter, and the input from the group has been extremely beneficial. My fellow authors have helped me with both the art and science of writing and storytelling. Thank you Shellie Arnold, Elizabeth Daghfal, Beth Gooch, Cindy Ervin Huff, and Mark Wainwright.

Speaking of people who make my work better, I am once again grateful for the feedback of my editor, Jessica Martin. She catches mistakes, tightens language, has great insight on characters, and generally brings both knowledge and wisdom to the process.

I am quite appreciative to all those who have purchased my books over the years.

I will be eternally grateful to the Author of all good things.

About the Author

Dr. Timothy Holder is a public speaker, radio show host/podcaster, author, professor, and actor. He makes appearances regularly on television, radio, podcasts, and in person, speaking primarily about presidents. His radio show/podcast, *The Leading Edge with Dr. Tim Holder*, airs in East Tennessee and West Virginia. It features interviews with leaders from a variety of fields. He is the author of many books, mostly on presidents or faith or both. He holds a Ph. D. in History and has served as a college dean in addition to teaching at both the college and high school levels. He has acted in commercials and movies and on TV, usually with his wife, the actress and producer Jill Holder.

www.ingramcontent.com/pod-product-compliance
Lightning Source LLC
Chambersburg PA
CBHW060648260626
47161CB00008B/3051